The killer was after Scarlet.

Again.

Jace entered Scarlet's room and found the security guard on the floor, clutching a stab wound.

Scarlet lay in her bed, her wild eyes darting back and forth.

Jace moved to her side. "You okay?"

"Tried. To. Smother. Me." Her words came in between ragged breaths.

"Who was your attacker?"

"Who are you?" She bit her lip. "Who am I?"

"Scarlet, you don't remember?"

She shook her head.

Lord, no! The assault must have given her amnesia.

The attacker had failed, but a thought bounced in Jace's pounding head.

The Coastline Strangler had targeted Scarlet Wells, and now she didn't know who she was or what the killer looked like.

Their only hope of determining CLS's identity had been ripped away—along with her memory.

Darlene L. Turner is an award-winning author who lives with her husband, Jeff, in Ontario, Canada. Her love of suspense began when she read her first Nancy Drew book. She's turned that passion into her writing and believes readers will be captured by her plots, inspired by her strong characters and moved by her inspirational message. Visit Darlene at www.darlenelturner.com, where there's suspense beyond borders.

Books by Darlene L. Turner

Love Inspired Suspense

Border Breach
Abducted in Alaska
Lethal Cover-Up
Safe House Exposed
Fatal Forensic Investigation

Visit the Author Profile page at LoveInspired.com.

FATAL FORENSIC INVESTIGATION

DARLENE L. TURNER

LOVE INSPIRED SUSPENSE
INSPIRATIONAL ROMANCE

LOVE INSPIRED® SUSPENSE
INSPIRATIONAL ROMANCE

ISBN-13: 978-1-335-72319-2

Fatal Forensic Investigation

Copyright © 2022 by Darlene L. Turner

Love Inspired
22 Adelaide St. West, 41st Floor
Toronto, Ontario M5H 4E3, Canada
www.LoveInspired.com

Printed in U.S.A.

But now, O Lord, thou art our father; we are the clay,
and thou our potter; and we all are the work of thy hand.
—*Isaiah* 64:8

For Mom and Dad Turner.
Thank you for your support and encouragement.
Love you.

Acknowledgments

There are always so many to thank when writing a book.

Suspense Squad sisters—
Dana, Shannon, Sami, Virginia, Loretta, Patty and Hope—
thank you for all the brainstorming and your friendships.
I'm grateful God put us together.

Thank you to Carrie Stuart Parks
for your expertise and advice on forensic art.

Chief Constable Ray—thank you for answering
my questions on Oak Bay and your department.

Tina James and Tamela Hancock Murray,
thank you for your continual guidance.

Jeff, you are my handsome PR guy. I love you.

Jesus, thank You for sculpting me in Your image.

ONE

The Coastline Strangler's face emerged one feature at a time on forensic artist Scarlet Wells's sketch pad. A tingle skittered down her arms, spreading into her fingertips as the creepy, evil eyes stared back at her. Eyes that would remain etched in her mind—forever.

Assigned to Vancouver Island's major crimes task force from Whitehorse, Yukon, Constable Scarlet Wells had arrived in Coral Bay, British Columbia, an hour ago and proceeded directly to the hospital to question Lila Canfield, the only witness to the serial killer's crimes. None of the other four victims had survived the killer's deadly grip on their throats. Lila shared that the man the news had deemed CLS had never spoken a word, which scared the woman the most. Had the eerie silence spooked Lila into forgetting vital details of her attacker's face? Scarlet had to get her to reveal more specifics to complete an accurate sketch in order to identify the killer taking innocent lives.

Scarlet needed a perfect sketch. So far, the witness had struggled with retelling her story as she lay paralyzed by terror on her hospital bed. No one would blame her after the ordeal she must have gone through. She'd barely escaped with her life. But Scarlet needed the woman to relax in order to proceed.

"You're okay, Lila. I'm here." Scarlet spoke in a hushed tone to calm the woman's nerves. She paused, waiting for Lila to take a breath. "Can you look at the facial features again in the book I gave you? It will help you remember CLS's face."

Lila recoiled, pulling her legs to her chest and folding her hands around her neck as if protecting herself from an unseen attacker. Fear returned and exploded in her widened eyes.

Scarlet put her pencil down, closed her sketch pad and moved closer to the bed. If she'd learned anything in the past seven years as a forensic artist, it was how to get a witness to trust her. Scarlet pulled Lila's hands away from her neck and took them in hers. "It's okay, Lila. I've got you. You're safe here. The team kept your condition confidential. The killer doesn't know you're alive."

Scarlet hoped she spoke the truth. With news of this serial killer running rampant, details could leak to the public easily through social media, no matter how hard the task force tried to keep them under wraps.

Lila flattened her legs on the bed and tugged the covers closer to her neck. "I just don't want to make a mistake and send the wrong person to jail."

"This is only a drawing of your memory. I won't let anyone innocent be arrested based on the sketch." Scarlet picked up her tools once again. "I need you to start at the beginning and leave nothing out, even if you think it's trivial. Everything is important."

Lila nodded. "Over the past few days, I've had an inkling someone was following me."

"Why did you think that?" Scarlet wrote Lila's exact words in her notebook.

"Just a sense. I can't explain it. Anyway, last night I went for a hike along the Bull Thistle Trail, and out of nowhere I felt a prick like a bee sting."

"Were there other hikers along the trail?"

"Yes, lots at that time of day. Within seconds, I was woozy and found myself falling. Someone caught me, and that's the last thing I remember before waking up with hands around my neck."

Scarlet wrote down Lila's words and "drugged?" beside them. Had the team found any indication of drugs in the other victims?

She squeezed Lila's hand. "You're doing great. What happened next?"

"I couldn't breathe and started to lose consciousness." She snapped her fingers. "Wait, I heard a noise, like someone stepping on a twig."

Something must have startled CLS. That's why the killer made a mistake by not ensuring Lila was dead. Scarlet wrote "find that person" beside Lila's quote of what happened.

"Could you tell where you were?" Not that Scarlet didn't already have that detail, but she wanted to find out if CLS usually killed his victims elsewhere.

"On a beach. I heard the waves and felt sand beneath me. He squeezed harder, and I passed out. The next thing I remember is waking up here in the hospital. God was looking out for me."

Scarlet flattened her lips as her fingers tightened around her pencil. God? Did Lila really believe that? Scarlet had once, but not after the night that robbed her of her faith. The secret she'd kept from everyone still haunted her after two years. She muzzled the memory and flipped a page in her facial identification book. "Can you pick out the shape of your attacker's nose?"

Scarlet spent the next two hours drawing the Coastline Strangler's face, revising along the way with Lila's modifications to the features of her attacker. "Last question, what did their hair look like?"

"Chin length, straggly, side-swept bang. I'm a hairstylist, so I remember that detail well."

Scarlet sketched the hair and held up her book. "Like this?"

Lila leaned forward, studying the face. "The nose is a bit wider."

Scarlet erased and made an adjustment. Moments later, she held it up again. "Better?"

Lila nodded as a tear escaped. "That's my attacker."

"You did great." Scarlet signed and dated her sketch. Now to take it to the task force. "Lila, can I get you—"

A fire alarm screeched.

Scarlet's pulse zinged, her muscles tensing.

Lila raised into a seated position. "Do we need to evacuate? I can barely walk."

"Let me check. I'll be right back." Scarlet dashed to the entrance and peeked out. The hallway was clear of fire or smoke. She veered toward the nurses' station as a masked patient-care worker brushed by and glanced at her for a split second before entering Lila's room.

Something about the person's expression niggled at her, but she failed to put her finger on it. She approached the bustling station and raised her creds. "Constable Scarlet Wells. Is this a fire drill? I'm interviewing Miss Canfield. Are we evacuating?"

The nurse nodded. "Yes, unless we find out otherwise. If you could help with Lila, we'd appreciate it. We're understaffed today."

She pointed toward the room. "But—"

Scarlet froze. The mention of Lila's name triggered a memory.

The Coastline Strangler's eyes.

The same eyes as the masked employee who'd just walked into Lila's room.

Scarlet sucked in a breath and turned to find the guarding officer's chair empty. Where was he?

She pounded the desk. "It's a false alarm. Call 911. Now! Lila is in danger." She fumbled for her weapon, but it wasn't at her side. Scarlet had stuffed it into her suitcase earlier, as she didn't want it exposed in the hospital. She barely ever used the nine-millimeter. *Stupid.*

Scarlet raced into the room and skidded to a stop at the entrance.

The masked attendant held Lila's flailing arms down as tremors shook her body.

"Get away from her!" Scarlet yelled.

The attacker looked in Scarlet's direction, giving Lila an opening to pull the mask down. Moments later, her body's convulsions worsened before her heart monitor flatlined.

Their only witness had just been silenced.

The attendant turned, withdrew a gun and pointed it at Scarlet.

The Coastline Strangler glared at her, smirking, before pulling the trigger.

Adrenaline kicked in and Scarlet dived, but not quickly enough to evade the bullet as it grazed her forehead. She stumbled into a table and whacked her head on the side, crumbling to the floor. Struggling to stay conscious, she lay still and prayed CLS would think her dead.

A ripping sound filled the room, and she squinted. CLS had torn a page from her sketchbook, thrown it into the garbage can and lit a match.

No! The sketch was vital for their investigation. However, she'd now seen CLS's face and would rely on her sharp memory to redraw the features. Once again, she closed her eyes.

Seconds later, stomping feet passed and exited the room.

More footfalls sounded.

She opened her eyes to see a uniformed man stopped in the entryway. Coral Bay police officer Jace Allen.

A man from her past. She wanted to tell him to run after the Coastline Strangler.

Her vision clouded as her head hammered. Scarlet raised her hand and pointed her index finger. She opened her mouth, but words failed to come out.

The stabbing pain increased. Her hand dropped, limp by her side.

Darkness enveloped her, hurtling her into blackness.

Smoke filled the private hospital room, assaulting Jace's nose. The fire alarm wailed, playing havoc with his migraine-prone head. He scrambled to Scarlet's side as the nursing staff bypassed him and ran to Lila. He guessed what they'd find—a deceased witness. How had the Coastline Strangler known she was alive? They had kept that information from the public.

Jace found Scarlet's pulse. *Thank You, God.* He yelled for help and dashed to locate a fire extinguisher. Finding one, he returned to the room and dispensed the foam into the garbage can. The flames extinguished, leaving only ashes and a tiny edge of paper. He used his pen and moved debris aside to get a better look. A name caught his attention.

Constable Scarlet Wells.

It was her composite sketch of the Coastline Strangler, but their killer's description was burned beyond recognition. Jace prayed Scarlet could remember details to recreate the person's face. It would be their only source of identification, since Lila Canfield was now dead.

Jace had suggested Scarlet's sought-after skills for their task force. She was the best of the best and what the team required to catch the Coastline Strangler. The serial killer had now taken five women's lives on Vancouver Island, mostly around the normally peaceful Coral Bay area. Jace's leader—Chief Constable Ray Carter—had tasked Jace to the major crimes unit and demanded he get the job done. This killer must be stopped.

Jace had immediately thought of Scarlet, his college crush, and after they'd found Lila alive, he'd requested his chief contact her. Jace wasn't sure if Scarlet would come if she'd known he'd been the source of the invitation for her to join the team. They had fought constantly in college, and those years had filled him with remorse and regret. However, that was in the past. Jace had become a new man after he'd given his life over to God.

"Step aside, Constable." A doctor knelt and began her examination of Scarlet.

Jace moved out into the hall and allowed the medical staff to take over. He dug his cell phone from his pocket and hit his chief's speed-dial number.

Hospital security arrived at the nurses' station and huddled together, discussing the situation.

"Carter here," the fiftysomething chief said. "What do you have for me, Allen?"

Carter's gruff voice hid his real persona of compassion for his officers and the residents of the tight-knit Coral Bay community.

"Bad news. Lila was killed and Constable Wells injured." He explained the attack and the fire that had obliterated Scarlet's sketch.

Carter huffed. "How did someone get by Constable Lewis?"

Jace noted the empty chair. "No idea. He's not at his post."

"Something's happened. Doug would never leave a witness unattended. Find him. Contact hospital security and ask them to check video surveillance. Remember what's at stake, Allen."

Leave it to the chief to remind him of his possible promotion if he solved this case. Weren't the lives of these women more important? "You mean keeping the public safe?"

A male attendant ran by with a gurney.

"That, too. Is Constable Wells awake?"

Seconds later, the doctor emerged, following the male attendant, who was wheeling the unconscious Scarlet on a bed.

"They're tending to her now. Gotta run. I'll update you later." Jace punched off and dialed Constable Lewis's number.

His coworker's *Star Wars* ringtone rang nearby. Jace followed the sound to a supply closet next to the victim's room. He unleashed his Glock 17 and eased the door open.

Constable Doug Lewis lay slumped in a chair, gagged and tied.

Jace cleared the tiny room, holstered his weapon and felt Lewis's wrist.

Steady pulse.

Jace gently nudged the constable. "Lewis, can you hear me?" He yanked the gag away.

The man stirred and slowly opened his eyes.

"Thank God, you're okay. What happened?" Jace untied the ropes.

Lewis rubbed his head. "I heard a crash behind the supply door and went to investigate. Got clocked from behind. Is Lila safe?"

"Afraid not. Killer took her out and attacked Constable Wells."

Lewis hung his head and mumbled, "It's all my fault."

Jace squeezed his shoulder. "You can't blame yourself, friend. This person is cunning, but how did they learn Lila was still alive?"

Lewis's jaw dropped. "Do you think we have a leak?"

Jace shrugged as heat kindled in his body. The thought of a fellow officer betraying them fueled his agitation. "Not sure. I'm hoping to get hospital security to check their video footage. You need to get examined." He helped him stand.

"I'm fine." Lewis's knees buckled.

"No, you're not. Come on." Jace led his coworker to the busy nurses' station. A security guard positioned himself to the side in a protective stance. Nurses huddled together, discussing their patients' conditions. Jace interrupted them and explained the constable had been attacked. They assured him they would look after Lewis.

Jace also inquired where they'd taken Scarlet. He memorized the room number and then approached the security guard, raising his badge. "I'm Constable Allen. You are?"

The slender guard shifted his feet. "Walt Watkins. How can I help you?"

"I'm investigating the victim's death and wanted security to check their video footage for any suspicious acts. Can you make that happen?"

Walt folded his arms. "I'll contact my superior."

"Thank you."

Walt unclipped his radio from his service belt. "Be right back." He walked around the corner and returned within minutes. "My leader said he'd check and then come see you. You can wait here." He gestured toward a small waiting room.

Fifteen minutes later, Jace sat next to Greg Webber—head of security—and waited for his report.

The tall man leaned forward. "I looked through the footage and noted a masked personal-care worker. That's not unusual, but their actions weren't normal. I first saw the person stuff something into their waistline upon exiting a patient's room. Then they brushed up against you on their way by." Greg held up his tablet. "But this caught my attention. I took a screenshot, as this reveals obvious danger."

Jace's pulse elevated. The enlarged frame revealed a Glock equipped with a suppressor.

"That's our suspect. You're saying they walked right by me?"

"Yes. I noted your uniform."

Jace slouched in his seat.

The Coastline Strangler had been so close and Jace hadn't realized it.

What kind of cop are you?

Jace rubbed his temples, massaging the sudden migraine emerging. *Not now.* He demanded focus, and the pain in his head wouldn't help the situation. He suppressed a groan, inwardly chastising himself. CLS had been within his grasp, and he'd let the suspect slip through the net. When his boss caught wind of his actions, it would squelch Jace's hopes of that promotion.

Shame on you for going there at a time like this. He shoved career thoughts aside and concentrated on his task. "Was the person a male or female?"

"Couldn't tell, as they were in full scrub gear."

"Did you find the suspect in any other footage?"

Greg shifted in his seat. "Not that same person, but I noticed something else. Not sure what made me stop the footage, but a masked doctor exited an office in scrubs. It appeared to be a woman, as they had longer hair, but her stance intrigued me. I come from a law enforcement background and know the signs. Her movements mimicked the earlier suspect, so I realized it was the same person. They hadn't left, but changed their appearance."

Why did that not surprise Jace? If this suspect was indeed CLS, the devious killer had eluded the police so far. They knew how to stay under the radar. "Is she still in the building?"

"Let me check the live footage." Greg picked up his tablet.

Jace's knee bounced as he waited for the man to review the cameras. *Stop being so impatient.* However, he couldn't help it. Lives were at stake.

Greg sat upright. "She just entered room A-503."

"That's Constable Scarlet Wells's room number. Get security there now!"

Jace flew out of his chair.

The killer was after Scarlet.

Again.

Jace unholstered his Glock and bolted out of the room, taking the steps two at a time to the fifth floor. He raised his weapon and opened the stairwell door. Loud noises filled the area.

Jace entered Scarlet's room and found the security guard on the floor, clutching a stab wound.

Scarlet lay in her bed, her wild eyes darting back and forth.

Jace moved to her side. "You okay?"

"Tried. To. Smother. Me." Her words came in between ragged breaths.

"Who was your attacker?"

"Who are you?" She bit her lip. "Who am I?"

What? She didn't know her own name?

"Scarlet, you don't remember?"

She shook her head.

Lord, no! The assault must have given her amnesia.

The attacker had failed, but a thought bounced in Jace's pounding head.

The Coastline Strangler had targeted Scarlet Wells, and now she didn't know who she was or what the killer looked like.

Their only hope of determining CLS's identity had been ripped away—along with her memory.

TWO

Scarlet opened her eyes, blinking several times to clear her murky vision, and peered around the dimly lit room. An irritating beep intruded on her tunnel-like hearing. Why did her head feel like she'd had a run-in with a truck? And more importantly—

Who *was* she?

The officer had called her Scarlet, but why couldn't she remember if that was her name? Adrenaline shot through her system, heightening her overwhelming sensation of dread. She lifted her hand to her forehead and fingered the bandage wrapped around her entire head. What *had* happened?

She attempted to sit. The beeps grew louder, elevating her pulse and ragged breathing.

"Whoa, now. Take it easy." The handsome blond police officer with the cute dimple gently guided her back down. "You're not going anywhere. Doc? She's awake again."

A petite woman stepped closer and shone a penlight in Scarlet's eyes. "Hold still."

Scarlet pushed the woman's hands away. "That hurts. What happened to me?"

"You don't remember?" the doctor asked.

"No. Who are you?"

"I'm Dr. Christine Beals. You were attacked. A bullet grazed your forehead, and when you fell, you hit your head. Hard."

"Why don't I remember?" How could her identity have been stripped from her so quickly?

Dr. Beals rolled the computer closer to the bed. "Can you tell me your name?"

Scarlet opened her mouth but clamped it shut again. She peeked at the officer. "He called me Scarlet. That's all I know."

The doctor typed on the computer's keyboard. "Your name is Scarlet Wells. What's your birth date?"

Scarlet racked her brain for a memory…any memory.

But none came.

Spots clouded her vision and increased her panicked state. The monitor beeped faster.

The doctor smiled. "It's okay. Take a breath. We'll figure this out."

Scarlet inhaled, then exhaled. Multiple times until her pulse slowed. "Why can't I remember?"

"You suffered a head trauma. Amnesia can happen after something like that."

"When will my memories return?"

The doctor glanced at the police officer.

Scarlet fisted the bedsheets in both hands and squeezed. "Doctor? What aren't you telling me?"

"We need to do further tests, but sometimes memories of trauma victims never return." She took off her stethoscope from around her neck. "Let's not go there yet, okay? I want to listen to your chest."

Dr. Beals placed the chest piece on Scarlet's heart and listened. "Strong. That's good." She turned to the officer. "She needs rest."

"Can I talk to her for a few minutes?" the officer asked. "I promise I won't be long."

"Okay. Scarlet, I'll ask the nurse to give you something in a bit to help you sleep. I'll see you in the morning." She didn't wait for a reply and exited the room.

The constable sat in the chair next to her bed. "Scarlet, do you remember me at all?"

She shifted her position to try to get more comfortable in the narrow hospital bed. "I'm sorry. I don't. How do we know each other?"

Sadness passed through his beautiful ocean-blue eyes. Somehow, this tugged at her heart. *Why?*

"College. Many years ago. My name is Jace Allen."

"Nice to meet you." She paused. "Again." She eyed a purse, a portfolio bag and a rolling suitcase in the corner of her room before turning back to him. "Did I travel here?"

He gazed at the luggage. "Yes. You live in Whitehorse, Yukon. You're here in Coral Bay to help with a criminal case."

Her jaw dropped. "What? How?"

He brought the purse and portfolio bag to her. "These might help explain. You're a forensic artist tasked to interview a witness who survived her attack. Do you recognize the name the Coastline Strangler?"

Suddenly, her shoulders tightened. Somehow the name struck her as familiar, but she couldn't recall any memory proving why. "Who is that?"

"A serial killer who's been targeting women on Vancouver Island. The last victim survived, and you came here this morning to interview her and draw CLS's face."

"Did I finish the sketch?"

Jace fished a bag from his pocket. "I believe you did, but it appears CLS burned it. When I got to the room, you were lying on the floor and your composite was burning in the garbage can. After putting out the fire, I found this. The only salvageable portion of what you drew." He handed it to her.

A piece of paper with a signature—*Constable Scarlet Wells*—and today's date.

She gave the evidence back to him. "Can you tell me exactly what happened to me?"

Scarlet's heart tightened during each part of Constable Allen's recounting of the story. At least, how he surmised it went down, including the unfortunate death of Lila Canfield.

Since her memory was erased and the sketch in ashes, how would they ever get a positive identification of the Coastline Strangler?

Tears pooled as a wave of coolness flushed her body. She wanted to be alone to think. To try to remember something.

Anything.

"I'm sorry, Constable Allen, but I'm tired and would like to rest now."

"Please call me Jace. I understand. My co-worker was hurt earlier, too, but checked by a doctor. He's back on duty outside your room for protection. I'll talk to you tomorrow." He paused and yanked a card from his pocket. "Call me if you need anything. Any time of day."

Their gazes held for a split second before he left the room.

Scarlet ignored the odd spark and picked up the portfolio. She opened it and flipped through the notepad.

Sketches of young and old faces, building structures, and scenery filled the pages. Impressive. *Did I actually draw these?*

She fingered the hard black pencil.

An image formed.

Haunting eyes.

She stiffened and dropped the pencil, slamming the portfolio shut. A question surfaced.

Did she want to remember?

For some reason, the pencil seemed like home, but it also brought a paralyzing sense of sadness and pain.

Why, she didn't know.

Jace walked into the Coral Bay police station's situation room and found it bustling even at the late hour. The task force had reconvened to discuss the case. He thought back to his conversation with Scarlet and the sadness in her eyes. He guessed she just wanted to be left alone in her own thoughts. Thoughts that probably were on the verge of recollection, but also far off at the same time. What would it feel like to forget everything from your past—including your own identity?

A shudder trickled through his body. He prayed he'd be able to help Scarlet regain her memory.

She was the key to solving the Coastline Strangler case.

But did Jace want her to remember his callous behavior during their college days?

Chief Constable Ray Carter walked into the room. His small stature hid the fact he was a force no one dared to challenge. "Jace, what news do you have?"

"Scarlet Wells has no recollection of the incident, CLS's face or her own past. From what we can tell, the head injury wiped her memory." He removed Lila Canfield's picture from a file sitting on the table. "Somehow, the killer knew Lila was still alive and eluded everyone at the hospital in order to kill her. We have no source of identification now. Back to square one." He added Lila's photo to the board beside the other four victims. "Also, Constable Lewis was attacked, but he is okay. He's on duty outside Scarlet's room until the end of shift. Any word on the security guard's injuries?"

"He'll make a full recovery. Walt said the attacker came out of nowhere and stabbed him. He didn't even see the person's face," Carter replied.

Jace paced, rubbing his tight muscles as he circled the room. "How did the killer find out Lila was still alive? Do we have a leak?"

The chief harrumphed. "Not in my house. No one would dare defy me."

Whitney Scott, Coral Bay PD's office assistant, hurried into the room and thrust an envelope in the chief's face. "This just came for you by delivery. I thought you'd want to see it right away. Look what's written on the front." She took a breath. "I only touched the corner."

Jace stepped closer and peered over Carter's shoulder.

You can't stop me.

The rough handwritten address also contained a sketch of a seashell at the bottom.

Carter whistled. "This is from the Coastline Strangler."

Jace turned to Whitney. "Who delivered it?"

"A boy on a bike. Once I read the front, I tried to catch him. But he was gone." She rubbed the bridge of her nose. "I'm sorry."

The chief shook his head. "Not your fault. Thanks for bringing it in so quickly."

"You're welcome." The short twentysomething assistant left the room.

Constable Gail Taylor slipped a notebook out of her vest pocket. "What does it say, Chief?"

Carter withdrew gloves from a desk drawer and put them on. He took a letter opener and sliced under the envelope's tab before gingerly removing the folded note. "'I will kill them all,'" he read. "'Just watch how close I can get to you.' It's signed CLS, with a seashell."

Behavioral analyst Peter Jones threw his hands in the air. "CLS is getting bolder."

Jace tapped his chin. "Agreed. CLS is taunting the police, similar to what other serial killers have done in the past. What does he mean by *get them all*? Get who?"

"The victims have been women." Taylor stood in front of the women's photos, fisting her hands on her hips. "The only thing we've determined is the killer targets the same type of woman—similar age and dark hair. Why?"

"Wish I knew," Jace said. "Something from CLS's past? Have we found any connections between the victims?"

Jones shifted his papers. "I haven't completed my profile yet, but no, we have found no similarities other than what Taylor indicated."

Jace let out an audible sigh. "There has to be something linking them together."

Jones turned to Carter and pointed to the note. "Chief, in my professional opinion, this proves CLS craves attention and I believe will use social media. We may want to set our phones to get alerts whenever the keywords *CLS* or *the Coastline Strangler* are referenced."

"Agreed. Everyone, please do as he says." Carter tapped on his cell phone's keyboard.

Jace entered the terms into their program as the others did the same.

Taylor ran her fingers along each woman's picture and then pivoted, her pretty hazel eyes flashing. "We need to protect them."

"But how? Scarlet's sketch was our only identification, and it's gone." Jace moved to the board and rearranged the pictures in order of their dates of death. "Let's go over the killer's MO again. The victims are strangled and then left on a beach with a string of seashells around their neck. What do you think it symbolizes?"

"No idea," Taylor said. "Why the beach?"

Jace rubbed his temples. "The beach is peaceful. Perhaps in CLS's warped mind, it's a resting place for the victim." He studied the dates of death. "The first two victims happened a year ago, six days apart. Victims number three and four, two weeks ago. Lila today. Why the break in killings?"

"Good question. Perhaps something triggered the recent attacks." Jones positioned himself beside Jace. "Who did you say was guarding the forensic artist?"

"You mean Scarlet Wells. She has a name, Jones." *Ouch.* Jace was tired and on edge. However, this constable had known how to get under his skin, ever since his affair with Jace's wife. *Get over it.* That was long ago, but Rene's betrayal still hit Jace hard whenever Peter Jones was in the same room. Jace checked his watch. "Constable Lewis is guarding her, but I suspect he's ready to go off duty. Any takers?"

"I'll go," Taylor replied. "She could probably use a woman right now."

"Makes sense." Jace gathered his belongings and stuffed them into a backpack. "My shift is done, too. I'm heading home. Need to tuck my son into bed. He probably forgets what his father looks like."

Charlie was his pride and joy. His five-year-old was the only good thing that came from his marriage before it ended in heartache. Well, that and his relationship with Christ. Rene Rockford had defied their vows when she'd cheated on Jace with Peter. Their affair had since ended and Rene had moved away, not wanting anything to do with her own son. Sad.

"Get some rest, Allen," his chief said. "We need to hit the ground running tomorrow to get more leads. Perhaps our community knows something. Canvass them again. Be safe."

"Understood. Night." Jace nodded at the other officers and headed out the front door to his personal vehicle.

The moon and stars glowed on the early-summer evening. Crickets sang, creating a peaceful atmosphere in the quaint town. Jace turned onto the road that would take him to his house, perched on a cliff with a walkway down to the beach, where Charlie loved to play in the waves and search for seashells. Wasn't that every child's favorite pastime?

Jace gulped in a breath. Wait—was that something the Coastline Strangler had done as a child? But why use the beach for such a horrific crime? Jace's grip on his steering wheel tightened. *Time to turn your mind off and tuck in your sweet boy.*

Jace smiled at the thought of Charlie wrapping his arms around Jace's legs as soon as he walked in the door—something Jace looked forward to every night after a hard day's work. However, the sudden desire to share his life with a woman materialized.

Scarlet's face popped into his head.

No. Stop. Remember your vow.

Neither he nor his son could take another betrayal.

Jace drove around the twisty road's curve and touched the brakes to slow down before the upcoming hill.

But his speed didn't change. He hit the brakes again.

Nothing.

The pulse in his head thrashed, his migraine returning full force.

His SUV picked up speed after another curve and headed downhill. He pumped the brakes again, but it was no use.

Watch how close I can get to you.

The Coastline Strangler's words came back to mind. Had CLS targeted the task force?

Jace struggled to maintain control as he hugged the double line, avoiding the steep right-hand ditch.

A car appeared from nowhere, and Jace swerved to dodge a collision. His tires caught the gravel on the road's edge and plunged him over the embankment. His vehicle flipped as his head jostled side to side and hit the window. Why hadn't his airbag deployed? The front windshield shattered and shards of glass showered into his vehicle's interior.

Jace prayed for safety with each rotation until he came to a stop at the bottom, next to the water. Any closer and he would have been submerged. A flame burst through his dented hood. He had to get out of the SUV. Now.

Lord, save me.

He grappled with his seat belt until it finally snapped open. Jace pushed on his door, but it was stuck. He scurried through the broken window. Blood dripped down his face and his head pounded as he crawled farther away from the fiery wreckage.

Jace had to call for help before he lost consciousness. Disoriented, he fumbled to retrieve his cell phone. Once he grasped the device, he dialed 911 and requested help—just before the flames engulfed the entire car.

His SUV exploded with a thunderous roar. The heat from the billow of fire intensified.

Jace retreated up the embankment, deeper into the overgrown beach weeds. He had to distance himself from the fiery inferno. Before he could take another step, his weary body succumbed to his injuries, and he dropped to the ground.

His vision blurred before his world turned black.

THREE

The next day after breakfast, Scarlet swiped through the pictures on her phone to see if they would dislodge memories. Anything to help remember CLS's face so they could identify the serial killer before he or she struck again. Women's lives were at stake. So far, nothing was working. "Ugh!" She tossed the phone on the bed.

Last night, she'd found the name Olive Wells on her list of phone contacts. On a whim, she called her and discovered Olive was her sister. She lived near Ottawa and worked as a criminal investigative analyst for the federal police. Their parents lived close to her. Olive promised to pray for Scarlet's amnesia to subside. A question had wedged in her mind since their conversation.

Did Scarlet believe in God?

Not knowing her identity brought another wave of rushing emotions, threatening to consume her body. She balled her fists as a breath seethed through her clenched teeth. *Stay calm.*

But how could she when she failed at remembering anything about herself? She wanted answers to the zillion questions running through her head.

Scarlet had also found out from Olive that Scarlet had sworn off men after her ex-boyfriend Brandon Snow hid his true identity. He had kept the fact he was married and had kids a secret. No wonder she didn't want to trust another man.

Scarlet pounded the bed. *Why can't I remember that?* She wanted to take her mind off herself, so she clicked the television remote's power button. A news break popped on the channel, with a caption below.

The Coastline Strangler targets the police force.

A plague of dizziness overtook Scarlet, and she pushed down the bile forming at the back of her throat. She needed to remember CLS's face. Frustration tightened her chest. She increased the volume to find out more details.

"Vancouver Island's task force members were targeted last night," the newscaster said. "Multiple officers are hospitalized, and one constable died from his injuries."

What? Was Jace okay?

"The Coastline Strangler is claiming responsibility," the anchorwoman continued. "Sources close to us say CLS sent a letter to the Coral Bay station, taunting the team."

Not good. Now CLS had targeted law enforcement. What would it take to stop this maniac?

Scarlet's cell phone buzzed. She shut off the TV and swiped the screen. It read *Sergeant Tobias Xander*. The name didn't ring a bell, but he was in her phone's contact list, so she hit Answer. "Scarlet here."

"Are you okay? Chief Constable Carter called and explained what happened."

She switched the phone to her other ear. "How do I know you?"

"Right, sorry. I heard about your amnesia. I'm Sergeant Xander, your leader in Whitehorse. You don't remember anything?"

Scarlet hit the speaker button and moved the phone away from her ear. "Nothing."

"What does the doctor say?"

"She's holding me until tomorrow for observation."

"Then what?"

"I'll probably head home to Whitehorse." *Home.* Where did she live? Condo? Apartment? Her lack of memory sent additional spikes of frustration through her already weakened limbs.

"They don't need you on the case?"

"What help am I?" Scarlet rubbed the bandage on her head. "I can't remember anything. I'm useless." There, she'd said what she'd been feeling. Out loud.

"You, young lady, are far from it. Search for

your name online and you'll see." A pause. "I will support whatever decision you make, but please don't lose hope. You've got this."

"Thanks, Sarge." Why did *Sarge* roll off her tongue so easily? Was that her normal response to him? A thought entered her mind. Did they have a close relationship? Perhaps he might help spark past reminders. "Can you tell me more about myself and what I do as a forensic artist? Am I a good employee?"

"Your duties include composite and age progression sketching, reconstruction, diagramming, plus you're trained as an officer, too." He paused. "You're the best at what you do."

Her stiff shoulders released. At least that was one relief. "Do I get along with my coworkers?" Why she asked that, she wasn't sure.

Silence.

What was he keeping from her?

"Sarge?"

Anxiety crept back into her body, tightening her muscles once again. "You still there?"

"I'm here. I just wasn't sure how to say this, but we've had a great relationship and always been honest with each other." He inhaled a loud breath. "Over the past two years, after your breakup with Brandon, you haven't been yourself. Been sharp to others. Closed off with me. That sort of thing."

She slumped in the bed. What warranted her

behavioral change? "I'm so sorry I've been like that. I wish I knew why. When did my relationship with Brandon end?"

"Two years ago. You grieved the loss hard, but something happened, and you suddenly became secretive. Then a bit hostile toward others. Some lodged complaints against you."

What? God, if You're out there, show me what I did so I can correct it.

Someone called her sergeant's name in the background. "Listen, I gotta run. It's gonna be okay. You are an amazing person, Scarlet Wells. Let me know if you need anything. Stay safe and keep me posted." He hung up.

Tears welled, and she let her phone slip from her fingers before burying her face in her hands. Sobs shook her body. Remorse filled her for the way she had treated others. She combed her brain to figure out what secret warranted her harsh attitude. *Why, Lord? Please show me what this secret is. Who am I?*

Search for your name online and you'll see.

She popped her head up as the words her boss had said earlier returned.

She wiped her face and took her tablet from her portfolio bag, bringing it to life. She typed her name into the search engine. Dozens of articles popped up, but one caught her attention.

Constable Scarlet Wells, Forensic Artist, Instrumental in Solving Cold Case.

She clicked the link and read. The article explained how she'd done facial reconstructions after officers found multiple skulls. These had helped identify the victims. Police were then able to link the female victims to a suspect who was later convicted. The young girls' families praised Scarlet for her outstanding work and thanked her for giving them closure after years of waiting with no word from their loved ones.

Wow. I did that?

She looked through the contents of her forensic bag—sketch pad, multiple pencils, erasers, fingerprint glass and a small notebook. She flipped it open and read, "Interview with Lila Canfield—Coastline Strangler survivor."

She'd taken notes. Why hadn't she thought to look at these last night when Jace gave her the portfolio? Perhaps they held a clue.

She read through her scribblings and stopped at her last notes at the bottom.

"I felt a prick like a bee sting. Within seconds, I was woozy and found myself falling."

Scarlet had written "drugged?" beside the quote. The last note said, "I heard a noise, like someone stepping on a twig."

Then Scarlet added, "Did a witness spook

CLS? Killer made a mistake by not ensuring Lila was dead. Find that person."

Scarlet slammed the book shut and fished out a business card from her wallet.

She had to call Jace Allen.

This information might be new to the case.

Maybe she could assist in the investigation after all.

Jace gripped his cell phone tighter and sat upright in his hospital bed. "Come again, Chief?"

Chief Constable Carter had called him this morning to give an update on the multiple attacks that had occurred last night. The paramedics had arrived in record time and whisked Jace off to the hospital. The emergency doctor wanted to keep him overnight for observation. Jace had disappointed his son when he told him he wasn't coming home, but Charlie's sixty-year-old live-in nanny, Marcy, would entertain him. Marcy was a gem and had now lived with them for three years. Jace promised Charlie popcorn and a movie to make up for his absence.

"Our team confirmed someone tampered with both your brakes and airbags. Plus, CLS sent another letter to the station, claiming responsibility for the attacks on our force last night and taunting us, saying we'll never stop the infamous CLS," Carter said. "The envelope also included a small seashell."

"We need to get a lead before more women are killed. Who else on the team was hurt?" Jace held his breath.

"A few injuries in other stations and Nanaimo's chief was killed. Thankfully, Gail only received minor scrapes and cuts. She's fine. Bad news on Jones. He died this morning from complications."

What? Heat crept up his neck, sending his rigid muscles into spasms. *Why such heartache, God?* Jace and Peter had their differences, of course, but Jace wouldn't wish this attack on anyone. He slouched in the bed and prayed for Peter's family. "How did the suspect get access to our vehicles without us knowing?"

"My guess is CLS probably tampered with your brakes while we were in our debriefing. The killer is smart and obviously knows cars. Not just anyone could do that so quickly. Or perhaps there's an accomplice."

"We need a break on this case—and fast." Jace's call waiting beeped in his ear. He checked the screen. *Unknown caller.* "Gotta go. Someone's on the other line. Contact me if you receive further information. The doctor is discharging me in a couple hours."

"Before you go, we're holding a press conference at 11:00 a.m. We need to reassure the public. Talk later." The chief disconnected.

Jace switched to the other call. "Constable Allen."

"Jace? It's Scarlet."

He shifted into a seated position. "What's wrong?"

"I found notes from my interview with Lila. There's something I need to share with you and the team. Can you come see me? I'm here until tomorrow."

The doctor entered his room.

"Actually, I'm also in the hospital. Had a car accident last—"

"You were one of the officers hurt by CLS? Are you okay?"

Her obvious concern for his welfare surprised him. Then again, she didn't remember their tenuous relationship all those years ago. "I'm fine. Bit of a concussion from where my head hit the window. Listen, the doc is here now, and I believe he'll discharge me today. I will come see you as soon as I can."

"Sounds good." She ended the call.

Jace tucked his cell phone away. "At least, I hope that's the case, Doc."

An hour later, after being officially cleared and discharged, Jace knocked on Scarlet's door. He peeked inside. "Permission to enter?"

"Of course," Scarlet said. "Come in, Constable."

"How are you feeling?"

"Bit better, but my memory is still foggy." She bit her lip. "Well, more than foggy—just gone."

"It will take time. What news did you want to share?" He moved a chair closer.

"Are you sure they should discharge you? I heard the news about the attacks."

He kept his balled-up fists in his lap. "I'm fine. A fellow officer was killed, so my mild concussion can't compare to what happened to him."

"I'm so sorry."

Jace ignored the pain in his head. "You said you found something in your notes?"

She opened a small notebook, flipped a few pages and handed it to him. "Yes. Look at the last couple of lines."

He read. Seconds later, his mouth dropped. "What? We may have a witness?"

"Yes, and it appears that CLS is drugging the victims first."

"It's possible this is the break we were waiting for. Excellent work. You're a valuable asset to our team."

"Hardly." She averted her gaze. "I'm probably going to return home. This amnesia has made me useless."

"That's not true, Scarlet." He paused. "You've done exceptional work in the past. Your policing and artist skills will kick back into gear. You know—like muscle memory."

"Maybe." She fingered her portfolio. "I thought you could plead to the public and ask this witness to come forward."

Jace checked the rest of her notes. "I need to run that by my chief first. We don't want to put that person at risk. I'm concerned we have a leak, because somehow CLS has been one step ahead of us. Speaking of that, there's a press conference starting now. Can we watch?"

She picked up the remote and turned on the television.

His chief and other task force members appeared. Carter gave an update on the investigation into the Coastline Strangler, leaving out details regarding the seashell necklaces found on the victims. The chief urged all women to be careful. He cautioned them to never go out alone, keep their doors locked and install alarm systems. He promised every officer would be deployed to watch over the community.

Reporters hammered the team with questions.

Seconds later, an alert sounded on Jace's cell phone. He checked his screen and popped to his feet. "What? CLS now has a social media account and is livestreaming this?"

A caption appeared across the livestream.

No woman can hide from me. I'm CLS and coming for you.

Jace looked at the TV. His leader ended the press conference.

Scarlet flicked off the television, squaring

her shoulders. "I'll stay, Jace. I can't leave these women without some type of hope. I just pray my memories return before it's too late."

Determination was etched on her beautiful face.

"I will help you however I can. I promise." He squeezed her hand. "Listen, do you need anything? A drink? A treat from the vending machine? Hospital food isn't always the best."

She smiled. "I would love a chocolate bar. Somehow I feel it's my downfall."

"One chocolate treat coming up." He left the room.

Fifteen minutes later, after searching the floor for a vending machine, Jace walked by the nurses' station.

A small card lay on the floor beside their counter. He scooped it up. "Someone lose this?"

The petite nurse's eyes widened. "Oh, that must have fallen out of Scarlet's flower bouquet. I delivered them a few minutes ago but took several big whiffs. I couldn't resist the gorgeous roses. Looks like she has an admirer."

Who else discovered she was here? His instincts told him to read the message.

He studied the card.

I won't fail this time, beautiful. xo.

Jace turned it over. A rough drawing of a small seashell appeared in the corner.

A crash sounded beside him.

The petite nurse collapsed to the floor, gasping for breath. Her back arched at a horrible angle.

Signs of poisoning.

No!

The flowers were tainted.

Jace bolted toward Scarlet's room.

He had to reach her before she sniffed the deadly bouquet.

FOUR

Scarlet lifted the roses someone had placed on the bedside table when she had fallen asleep in the short time since Jace had left to find chocolate. Crashes sounded outside her room, and she startled at his sudden appearance as he catapulted toward her at full speed. The contorted expression on his handsome face sent tremors tumbling through her body. "Jace, what's—"

He swatted the flowers from her hand. "Poison!"

The glass vase hit the floor with a deafening explosion, shattering into pieces. Water spewed everywhere.

Scarlet's jaw dropped.

Jace took her hands in his. "Are you okay? Did you smell the bouquet?"

"No, but I was about to. What's going on?"

"CLS got to you again." He gestured toward the flowers. "Laced the roses with some type of poison."

"What? How do you know?"

Jace handed her a card. "Found this on the floor outside your room, and the nurse told me she smelled them before bringing them to you. Minutes later, she collapsed."

Scarlet read the card. Her fingers trembled, and she almost dropped the note after realizing the message was intended for her eyes only.

"Check the back," Jace said.

She flipped it over. A small seashell sketched in the bottom right corner caught her attention. CLS's signature. She clamped her hand over her mouth, but not in time to quench her sharp intake.

The killer continually evaded the police. How?

A scurry of pounding feet outside her room interrupted her thoughts. "What's going on? Is the nurse okay?"

His shoulders sagged. "The other nurses were working on her, but it didn't look good."

This attack meant one thing—the killer was still targeting Scarlet, and Jace had saved her life.

Again.

Scarlet fisted her hands. This person needed to be captured and put behind bars. Obviously, CLS wouldn't stop coming after her, so she was determined to remember the killer's face.

A question emerged. "Jace, CLS knows I'm still alive but doesn't realize I'm not a threat since I lost my memory. Should we publicize that fact? Would that stop the killer's pursuit of me?"

He raked his fingers through his blond hair. "I doubt it."

She touched his arm. "Thank you for saving my life. Again."

His eyes caught hers and held for a second.

Scarlet snapped her hand away and averted her gaze, a question forming in her mind. Had there been some type of spark between them in college?

If so, something had severed it. Scarlet searched her brain to remember, but nothing came.

"I'm going to talk to your doctor. We have to get you released so we can protect you better."

"I don't understand how someone—"

A flurry of nurses scurried into her room, with Dr. Beals in tow, interrupting their conversation. The group stopped at the sight of the shattered glass and discarded roses.

"I'll get a broom," one nurse said and exited the room.

"Sorry for the mess." Jace moved away from Scarlet. "She was about to smell the roses, and I had to stop her quickly. My guess is they were poisoned."

Dr. Beals nodded. "Agree. The nurse had symptoms, but we'll know more once the coroner does an autopsy."

Another nurse adjusted Scarlet's IV and checked

the monitor before inputting information into the mobile computer.

Scarlet swallowed, pushing down the rising nausea. "She's dead because of me." She massaged her temples and fought back the tears forming. The thought of someone dying in her place not only overwhelmed her but shot darts of fury through her heart. This had to end. Now.

Jace waggled his finger in her direction. "No. CLS did this. It's not on you, Scarlet." He turned to the doctor. "Dr. Beals, she's not safe in this hospital and needs to be under police protection. Can you release her?"

The doctor tapped her foot as if in consultation with herself. "She's had serious trauma to her head, Officer. It's not just a mild concussion."

"I get that, but weren't you going to release her soon, anyway?" Jace stepped closer. "Between us, CLS somehow knows our moves. We need to remove her from the equation so we can concentrate on catching this criminal before they kill again. Women's lives are at stake."

"I understand, but my patient's life is as well. I can't risk her health."

"Hello, I'm right here." Scarlet waved. "Dr. Beals, I agree with Jace. I'm feeling better today. Still weak, but I'll be okay. I need to protect other women by helping to find this killer." Scarlet now realized even without her memory, she would stop at nothing to bring this person to justice.

She wouldn't have more women's deaths on her conscience.

Dr. Beals groaned. "I'm outnumbered here. Let me do another thorough examination, and then I'll consult with my medical team before the end of shift."

Scarlet shimmied higher in her bed. "Thank you. I'd rather leave with your blessing than on my own accord."

The nurse returned with a broom.

Jace ran to her side. "Wait, I need to gather the flowers for Forensics to examine. Do you have a large plastic bag?"

She nodded and once again exited.

Two hours later, after Dr. Beals cleared Scarlet and Jace had dropped off the flowers at the station, he parked in the driveway of a beach cottage owned by a friend. The chief had assigned Constable Gail Taylor to Scarlet's protective detail, and she sat on the steps, her arms crossed and duffel bag at her feet. Clearly, she was not happy to be Scarlet's bodyguard.

Scarlet turned to Jace. "Do you really think I need a babysitter? I can take care of myself."

Jace shut the engine off. "I'm sure you can, but we're not taking any risks. CLS has targeted you."

"She doesn't look happy to be here."

"Taylor can be rough around the edges, but she's a good cop." He opened his door. "Let's go."

Scarlet stepped out of his vehicle and breathed in the ocean air. The waves slapped against the shore, greeting her with a sense of home and happiness. Had she also lived close to a beach? Olive hadn't mentioned their childhood house, but a sense of peace washed over Scarlet as soon as she exited the car. Hopefully, a walk on the beach would be on her itinerary at sunset. Perhaps it'd clear her mind and give her insight into her past.

A pregnant, redheaded woman opened the door and bounded down the steps. "Scarlet, I presume? I'm Violet. Welcome to my oasis. You will love it here."

Scarlet breathed in again, lifting her face to the late-afternoon sun. "I already do. I can't believe you had an opening."

"A family just canceled an hour before Jace sent me a text."

Jace pulled her suitcase from the vehicle. "That's what I like to call a God thing."

Did he believe, the same as Olive? That an unseen entity watched over their lives? The question Scarlet would like to know was…did she?

She shrugged it off and picked up the rest of her belongings from the front seat. "I'm not sure about that, but I appreciate you letting me stay here."

Constable Taylor stood. "It's secluded, and I will keep you safe." She turned to Jace. "I've done a sweep of the property. All clear."

"Good, thanks," Jace said. "Glad to see you're okay after your accident."

Violet walked back up the steps and opened the screen door. "How long will you be here, Scarlet?"

Scarlet hugged her portfolio to her chest as if it would protect her from harm. "I'm not sure yet. Will depend on the case we're working on."

Scarlet entered the midsize cottage. A coconut scent embraced her, sending more peaceful thoughts through her mind. *Yes, I will love it here.* Then, without warning, a swirl of trepidation snaked through her body. Images of children at a bonfire formed, along with a powerful blast. Previous peaceful beach thoughts turned to waves of terror. Her legs buckled, and she grabbed the nearest wall to steady herself. How could the beach bring both peace and panic, all in one emotion? Was this what the women went through before CLS strangled them? Or was this a memory that had nothing to do with the case?

Jace dropped her suitcase and moved closer. "You okay? Breathe."

Scarlet inhaled and exhaled slowly multiple times.

Violet rushed from the entryway into the kitchen and returned with a water bottle. "Here. Drink."

Scarlet obeyed. Finally, the moment of terror subsided.

"What happened? Is it related to the case you're working on?" Violet asked.

Scarlet lifted her brow. They couldn't talk about the case.

Jace turned to Violet. "I think Scarlet needs to rest. Can you leave the key and I'll chat with you later?"

The woman's pretty green eyes clouded as she bit her bright coral lips. She took keys out of her pocket and hung them on the hook by the door. "Sure. I hope you feel better, Scarlet." She turned to Jace. "Please call me later. I need to tell you something." She didn't wait for a response, but left the three-bedroom cottage. The screen door slammed in her wake.

Clearly, Jace's dismissal of Violet annoyed her. What was the pregnant woman's story?

Scarlet had noted Violet's empty ring finger. "Thanks, Jace. I'm not sure what information she was fishing for, but obviously we can't discuss an ongoing case."

"She's friendly, but a bit of a busybody. Sad about her situation, though." Gail plunked her duffel bag on the laminate floor. "I'm going to go check out the rooms." She walked down the corridor.

Curiosity niggled at Scarlet. "What situation?"

"Violet went to a bar a few months ago and woke up the next morning at home with no memory of her evening. She's a forensic toxicologist and ran a tox screen on herself. She discovered drugs in her system. Weeks later, she found out she was pregnant."

Tears formed, weakening her limbs. Scarlet sank onto the plush tan couch. "Wow. I'm so sorry." Why was this rush of emotion plaguing her over Violet's condition?

"She's like a kid sister to me." Jace sat on a dining room chair. "Change of subject. Were you having some type of memory flash or a dizzy spell from your head trauma?"

"Not sure. I think it might have been from my childhood, but a thought crossed my mind. Why would CLS use a place like a peaceful beach to kill the women? Does it have some sort of connection with CLS's childhood?"

Jace peered at his watch. "Good questions, but for now, you need to rest. Tonight and all day tomorrow. Taylor will be with you."

"But—"

He raised his hands. "No arguments. Tomorrow evening, I'll bring you to my beach house for a BBQ. I want you to meet someone."

A twinkle formed in his ocean-blue eyes.

Did he have a girlfriend or fiancée he wanted Scarlet to meet?

She swallowed the jealousy forming. *Stop it.* "Sure. Where's your house?"

Jace walked to the window. "Up there." He pointed.

Up?

Scarlet followed the direction of his finger. A large home built on the cliff above the beach stood proudly. She whistled. "That's *your* house?"

"Well, it was my parents'. They left it to me upon their deaths."

Scarlet noted the pain still etched on his rueful face. "I'm so sorry."

"Thanks. Normally, you could walk from here, but you're still weak, so I will pick you up at six o'clock tomorrow, okay?"

"What about the case?"

"The team will follow up with other stations and compare notes. Get some rest. See you tomorrow." He left.

Scarlet once again stole a peek at the mansion built into the cliff and wondered what his parents had done for a living to afford such a luxurious home.

Gail returned to the living room and scooped up her duffel bag. "I'll take the first bedroom. The one at the rear is more secluded for you."

"That's fine. I appreciate all your help."

"Let's get something straight right off the bat." Gail's eyes darkened. "I was ordered to be here. It was not by choice, and I will not babysit you." She stomped down the hall.

Ouch. What had she done to deserve Gail's anger?

She had to deal with not only a killer targeting her, but now a bodyguard who despised her for some odd reason.

The next evening, after he picked up Scarlet, Jace drove through the wrought iron gate and down the long, paved driveway of his cliff house, often referred to as "Coral Bay's beach mansion." He'd hated that name all his life. His friends confessed to being jealous of his parents' wealth and soon snubbed him as the spoiled rich boy. At one point, he *was* that boy, but during his college years, he'd had his eyes opened after a drunk driver killed his parents.

His brother, Heath, had challenged him to mend his ways and start acting his age. Heath had even threatened to disown him as a brother. That hit Jace hard. He'd mended his ways and gone into law enforcement. Best decision he'd made, as his job instilled and engrained in him a better attitude. He now lived by the serve-and-protect motto daily. His regimen, along with his Christianity, gave him purpose in life.

If only that purpose also included a woman to share his life with, but Rene had stripped his faith and trust in women with her betrayal. He stole a peek at the raven-haired beauty beside him, and a question rose. Was she different from the other women he'd dated? More importantly, would she forgive him once she remembered the last harsh words they had exchanged in the college library that night years ago?

Jace rounded the bend, and his home came into view.

Scarlet's sharp intake of breath didn't surprise him. It was how most people reacted to his parents' home.

"Wow. I can't believe you live here."

He hit the opener and drove into the three-car garage. "I couldn't bring myself to sell it, as all my childhood memories are here. My brother had moved away by the time our parents died and made a life for himself in Ontario. We co-owned it until he passed."

Scarlet squeezed his hand. "What? I didn't realize you were alone."

"Heath was a border patrol officer and helped put away a Buffalo crime family. They put out a contract on his life, and he was killed a few months ago."

"I'm so sorry."

"But I'm not alone. I have someone special in my life." Charlie gave Jace constant joy. A reason to come home happy every night after work, even after his wife's betrayal.

Scarlet's gorgeous brown eyes stood out against her bright blue blouse. He could get lost in her gaze.

Stop, Jace. Move on. He cleared his throat and opened the door. "Shall we?"

"Yes."

He led her to the side door into his home. Jace had invited Taylor to come along for supper, but she'd refused and stated she'd keep the cottage safe from perpetrators while Scarlet was gone.

The pitter-patter of tiny feet sounded on the shiny marble floor. Seconds later, his bouncing, curly-haired blond boy came around the corner.

"Papa!"

Once again, Scarlet took in a sharp breath beside him.

"Scarlet, I would like you to meet my son, Charlie." Jace tousled his five-year-old's curls. "Charlie, this is my friend, Miss Scarlet."

Charlie's blue eyes widened. "You have pretty hair."

Scarlet squatted. "Why, thank you. It's nice to meet you, Charlie."

Charlie's nanny, Marcy, walked down the corridor, wiping her hands on her buffalo-plaid apron. "Good evening, Scarlet."

"This is my amazing nanny and housekeeper, Marcy. She lives with us." Jace couldn't have gotten through these past few years without Marcy Kendricks. She'd been his rock in the hard times.

"Nice to meet you, Marcy," Scarlet said.

"You, too. Supper will be ready in twenty minutes. I hope you like BBQ turkey steaks." Marcy gestured toward Jace. "His fave."

Scarlet laughed. "Sounds delish."

Marcy retreated down the hall.

"Miss Scarlet, come." Charlie took her hand and tugged her forward. "Come see my toys."

"Son, be careful. She just got out of the hospital."

Charlie dropped her hand. "You sick? What's wrong with your head?"

Scarlet touched the bandage. "I'm okay. Just bumped my noggin. What did you want to show me?" She winked at Jace before following Charlie down the hallway.

An hour later, the group sat around a roaring bonfire. Charlie had insisted Jace start a fire early so he could roast a marshmallow for his new friend, Miss Scarlet. His son had since stuffed two into his mouth, along with a s'more. For some strange reason, Scarlet had placed her lawn chair farther away from the fire, distancing herself.

"Son, say good night. Time for you to get ready for bed."

Marcy stood and held out her hand. "Let's go, bud."

Charlie ran to Scarlet and threw himself into her arms. "Night, Miss Scarlet. Will you come back and play with me tomorrow?"

She giggled. "We'll see, Charlie. Have a good sleep."

His son held Marcy's hand as he bounced toward the patio doors.

"He's adorable. If you don't mind me asking, where's his mother?" Scarlet stuffed an unroasted marshmallow into her mouth.

"Out of the picture for good." Jace didn't mean for his tone to come out harsh, but there were still times when Rene's betrayal hit him hard.

Scarlet averted his gaze. "I'm so sorry."

He stared at the horizon. The sun had moved closer to the skyline, and the view from his backyard cliff took his breath away every night. In all the different seasons. Sun rays bounced off the water, spreading through the ripples. "She's been gone for three years now."

"Doesn't she visit Charlie?"

"Nope. Sad, isn't it?" He kicked at an escaped ember. "I'm pretty sure Charlie doesn't remember his mother. He was only two when she—"

He stopped midsentence. Was he ready to trust another woman with his personal life?

No, not yet.

Jace threw a stick in the fire. It ignited, and flames shot upward.

Scarlet recoiled in her lawn chair.

"What is it?" Jace asked.

"The fire startled me." She tugged a cardigan on and looked away.

Jace sensed it was something far worse, but was that lost in her amnesia, too? He rubbed ash from his fingers. "Listen, I best get you back to the cottage. You need another good night's rest."

She nodded. "I want to meet the team tomorrow."

"Will you feel up to it? The doc wouldn't like you returning so soon after being released." Jace sprayed water on the fire. It sizzled before extinguishing the flames.

"I'll be fine. I need to help catch CLS. Women are depending on me, and I won't let them down." The angst in her raspy voice came out loud and clear.

She meant business and obviously wouldn't back away from this case.

Plus, the team required her expertise.

If only she could remember CLS's features to obtain an identification.

Before the Coastline Strangler struck again.

Scarlet stood on the cottage's patio, mesmerized as the summer sun kissed the shoreline with a spectacular display of pink, orange and violet. Crickets chirped in surround sound. *I could get used to this view and ambience.* Gail was close by, guarding her, hand resting on her weapon. Scarlet had argued she was safe and wanted to be alone, but Gail refused to shirk her duties. Scarlet understood and didn't argue the point further.

She thought back to her evening with Jace and his son. Scarlet had caught the anger in Jace's eyes when she asked about Charlie's mother. Clearly, the woman had inflicted damage on Jace's heart. Scarlet wanted to learn more, and he'd been about to say something, but he had clammed up. *None of your business.*

However, Scarlet found it hard to ignore the spark between them. And Charlie? He'd already stolen her heart.

Her cell phone jingled a tune. She fished it from her pocket and swiped the screen. Olive. "Hey, sis."

"How are you?"

"Coming along. I'm under protective detail. We're at a cottage down the beach from Jace's mansion. You should see his place. And Olive? He has an adorable five-year-old son, Charlie. Such—"

"Slow down, Scarlet. Be careful."

"I will not fall for Jace. We're coworkers. That's all. Tomorrow, I meet the team."

"Are you sure you should work?"

"I rested today and I'm ready. I need to protect these women, Olly." Wait—was that her nickname for her sister? It rolled off her tongue too easily.

"Sounds like your memory might be returning. You've called me Olly ever since you were four."

The flashback of children sitting around a fire returned. "I also remembered something else. Well, I'm not sure what it represents."

"What?"

"I remember children at a bonfire with firecrackers. Only, it didn't seem like a happy occasion."

Olive groaned. "It wasn't. Your fear of fires started that day."

"My what?"

"You were nine, and you and your best friend, Becky, wanted to make s'mores, but it had just rained, so your fire wouldn't start. You found Grandpa's diesel can but placed it too close to the fire. You ran off to get the marshmallows from the house and when you came back, the can exploded. You were hurt, but Becky was killed."

Scarlet's legs buckled, and she collapsed to the wooden deck. "What? I killed my best friend." *It was my fault. How could I have been so stupid?* No wonder she'd felt the need to sit away from the fire tonight.

"Scarlet, it was an accident. You were too young to realize what could have happened."

Pain stabbed through her chest, as if she was back at the beach all those years ago. The horror she must have gone through overwhelmed Scarlet. "I knew the memory was dark. Did we live on the beach?"

"No, Grandma and Grandpa did. We visited them every summer. Why?"

"When Jace brought me here, I had this overwhelming sense of peace when I stepped out of the car. The ocean smell and waves soothed my anxiety."

Olive chuckled. "That's because you loved your summers with them and spent most of your time digging for clams."

Scarlet eased herself into a standing position. "Too funny." She rubbed her throbbing head. "Listen, I need to turn in. Can we chat tomorrow?"

"Of course. Night, sis. Love you."

"You, too." Suddenly, she knew that to be true. Even though she didn't remember her sister, she felt their strong bond.

Seagulls squawked in the distance.

She turned toward the ocean and caught a flock flying into the sunset in a perfect V formation. The air's stillness soothed her, and the birds did, too.

Her cell phone buzzed. She swiped and read the screen.

You can run, but you can't hide from CLS. I will find you.

Trepidation crawled between her shoulder blades, inching throughout her entire body. So much for stillness and thoughts of a good night's sleep.

It was vital the team catch this person before CLS found them.

FIVE

Jace held the Coral Bay police and fire station door for Taylor and Scarlet. Taylor dashed down the hall and into their lunchroom, probably getting her normal morning coffee fix. He followed Scarlet and caught a waft of strawberry and vanilla as she walked into the building. Jace tried to ignore the intoxicating scent but failed miserably. He had to halt any further thoughts and concentrate on the case, especially after she'd told him about CLS's text. They'd tried to determine how CLS had gotten her unlisted number but only hypothesized that the killer must have somehow obtained it from her medical records during her hospital stay. Jace had the sudden urge to do anything to protect his college friend, even when he knew their relationship would never turn romantic. He owed her that much.

As if sensing his thoughts, she turned. "You're awfully quiet this morning."

"Sorry. Lots going through my mind." He gestured to the right. "The team's briefing room is this way."

"How many are on the task force?"

"Lots in different locations across Vancouver Island. Including you and me, we have six here." He winced. "Make that five. We lost our behavioral analyst in the attack against our team."

She rubbed his arm. "I'm so sorry."

Her touch sent electric currents tingling through his body.

She dropped her hand.

Had she felt it, too, or was it because they had entered the bustling room?

Whatever the answer, Jace ignored the spark and whistled to get everyone's attention. "Folks, I want to introduce you to Scarlet Wells. As you are aware, she's here to help with the identification of the Coastline Strangler. She's trained in both forensic art and policing."

Constable Doug Lewis stepped forward. "We never officially met at the hospital. I'm Constable Lewis."

She nodded. "Nice to meet you. How are you feeling?"

He rubbed his forehead. "I'm fine."

The chief huffed. "Hardly. I told Lewis he should stay home another day, but he's determined to defy orders."

Lewis grimaced. "CLS got by me on my

watch. I'm determined to bring this person to justice."

Jace appreciated the man's perseverance. "Scarlet, this is our leader, Chief Constable Ray Carter."

"Glad to have you with us, Constable Wells." He held out his fist.

She bumped it with hers. "Thank you. Call me Scarlet, please."

Jace pointed to a slender constable leaning against the wall. "That's Frank Heller, federal police constable. He was just tasked to our team."

Heller nodded.

Constable Taylor sauntered into the room, coffee in hand.

"Of course, you've already met Constable Taylor," Jace said.

The chief clapped. "Grab a coffee and we'll start in five." His cell phone jangled, and he swiped the screen. "I gotta take this."

Jace pointed to the door. "The machine is in the break room down the hall on the right."

"You don't want any?" Scarlet asked.

"Hate the stuff. Plus, I already drank my cup of Earl Grey. You go ahead."

"What? You don't strike me as a tea drinker." She lifted her pinkie, chuckled and exited the room.

Six minutes later, Jace stood in front of their case board. "We now have five victims, and we're no further ahead." He ran his fingers through his hair and reeled in his frustration. "CLS somehow knows our every move. If someone from this team is leaking information, we will find you out." He broadened his stance, eyeing each team member. He hated to push any authority over the team, but Scarlet's safety and that of the women of their community were at risk. He could no longer play Mr. Nice Cop.

Heller stepped into Jace's personal space. "How dare you accuse one of us Maybe it's you, Mr. Spoiled Rich Guy. Yes, I'm new to the team, but I've already heard about your fancy house."

Jace silenced his irritation. When would people stop thinking he was rich? If only they realized he'd put the majority of his parents' money into a trust fund for Charlie and Jace was living off his own salary.

"He has a point, Allen. How do we know it's not *you*?" Taylor took a sip from her Coral Bay PD mug, her hazel eyes boring through him.

Jace and Taylor had clashed from the first time they'd met, but he'd worked hard to shift their rocky relationship into a friendship. However, Taylor refused to budge.

Carter clucked his tongue. "Enough. This team is rock-solid. I trust each of you. Let's move on." He glared at Jace.

Message received. *Give it a rest and figure out who's really behind this.*

Scarlet moved to the board and traced each woman's picture as if trying to get close to them. "Do we know whether CLS is male or female yet?"

"No." Jace checked his notes. "Hospital security confessed when they saw the video footage, they thought it was a male, but it later appeared the suspect disguised their appearance and CLS's movement seemed feminine." He flipped a page. "Scarlet, I mentioned to the team what you discovered, but I want them to hear it from you. Tell them what you found in your notes from Lila's interview."

Scarlet cleared her throat and opened her portfolio. "Lila told me she heard a branch snap, so someone may have witnessed CLS strangling her."

A collective gasp filled the room.

"Did she see anyone?" Taylor asked.

"No. She also felt a prick like a bee sting and immediately felt woozy before blacking out. Sounds like she was drugged." She addressed the chief. "Have you received tox screens back from the other victims?"

"Let me check." Carter typed on his laptop. "Yes, on the original two victims, but nothing showed up in their systems. This is good information. Once we have our profile, we'll add the witness to our press conference and ask them to come forward."

"We need that profile," Lewis said. "However, with Jones gone, it will be hard. He had a keen eye for detail with his specialized training."

Scarlet eyed the note CLS had sent to the station. "Jones?"

"Constable Peter Jones, the behaviorist I mentioned earlier that died from the targeted hit." Jace addressed his leader. "Chief, any word on a replacement?"

"I've put feelers out," Carter said.

"Wait. I have an idea." Scarlet brought out her cell phone. "Does the person need to be present to give a profile?"

"It would be good but not totally necessary." Carter closed his laptop. "What do you have in mind, Scarlet?"

"My sister, Olive, works in the same field. She may help if you send her all the files."

"Where does she live?"

"She works for the federal police in the Ottawa area." Scarlet held up her phone. "Do you want me to call her?"

Jace placed his hands on the table, leaning into it. "Carter, do you have the authority to make that decision for the joint team?"

"I do as of this morning. That phone call earlier was from the Major Crimes Unit's sergeant. He's appointed me task leader after Chief Constable Powell was killed in the hit."

Jace balled his fists, quenching the urge to

pound the table. It was essential they get in front of this investigation instead of trailing behind. "There have to be other suspects working with CLS. Powell was stationed in Nanaimo."

"We thought we were only dealing with one perp." Carter tapped the table. "Scarlet, call your sister."

Scarlet hit buttons and placed her phone in front of the group.

Her sister answered on the first ring. "Hey, sis. How's it going today?"

"Olive, I have you on speakerphone here at the Coral Bay police station with the task force," Scarlet said. "We need your expertise."

"Okay. How can I help?"

"Hi, Miss Wells. This is Chief Constable Ray Carter. Our team is down a behavior analyst, and Scarlet here says you could help provide a profile on our killer."

"I would need to check with my leader first, because I'm working other cases at the moment. If he approves, I would be honored, sir."

"Give me his name and number. I'll call and explain the situation." Carter wrote on a nearby sticky note. "If he approves, where can I send the files to get you up to speed?"

Olive recited her leader's name and phone number and her own email address.

Carter tore the note off. "We'll be in touch. Thank you."

"Of course. Scarlet, chat with you later?"

"Sure thing." Scarlet ended the call.

Jace moved back to the case board. "In the meantime, we—"

Pounding feet cut off his statement.

Whitney, their office assistant, darted into the room. "Chief, just got a call. Another woman was found. This time on Thistle Beach."

Jace sprang to his feet, his pulse thrashing in his head.

The Coastline Strangler had struck again—this time closer to home.

Scarlet sidestepped the multiple driftwood logs and inched carefully toward the Coastline Strangler's latest victim. Could she do this? How many bodies had she seen in the past? Her lost recollections failed to answer that question. She clutched her portfolio to her chest as if it would protect her from harm—her safety blanket. The sketch pad felt like home in her hands. How could she know that but couldn't remember CLS's face? She took another step but hesitated. *You can do this. You have to do this.* The women of Vancouver Island were depending on her. She moved closer.

Jace gently guided her away from the body and placed his hands on her shoulders, turning her to face him. "You can sit this one out, but I need you to stay close, since CLS is still after you."

She looked into his eyes. Eyes that matched the water in front of them. His protective nature reached into the depths of her heart. Her gaze moved to the dimple on his chin. She raised her hand but dropped it, resisting the urge to explore what it felt like. *Concentrate.*

She stepped back. "I'm okay. I have to do this." She gestured toward the woman. "For her. For them. My boss told me I've done some crime scene diagramming in the past, so I'm going to attempt that."

Jace placed his hand at the small of her back. "Take it slow. Perhaps a memory will return. Let's check our victim out, shall we?"

They moved together toward the body.

The woman lay in a peaceful pose, her arms folded across her chest and hands arranged in a prayer formation. A string of seashells partially hid the red ring around her neck. Did the killer think the necklace would conceal her cause of death?

Two coroners huddled over the body, examining the woman inch by inch. Part of the team scoured the area for clues while the others pushed the crowd behind the yellow caution tape, questioning witnesses.

"Scarlet, I would like you to meet our coroners," Jace said. "This is our chief coroner, Dr. Henry Drew. This is forensic artist Constable Scarlet Wells."

The two men stood.

Dr. Drew extended his hand. "Nice to meet you."

Scarlet returned the gesture. "You, too."

Dr. Drew once again stooped down in front of the victim but gestured to the younger of the two coroners. "This is my right-hand man, deputy chief coroner, Dr. Aiden Parker."

"It's a pleasure, Miss Wells, but call me Aiden." Aiden slipped off his black-framed glasses and stuffed them into his front pocket. "Do you normally come to crime scenes?"

"My leader told me I sometimes assist, but not always. Constable Allen wanted me to stay close for protection." Scarlet examined the two coroners. Both around the same age. Both smaller in stature. "Does British Columbia always send two coroners to a scene?"

Dr. Drew pulled forceps from his medical bag. "Sometimes, but Aiden here has been working alongside me for a couple of years now, learning the ropes. He will take over soon as the chief coroner, because I'm moving to New Brunswick to be closer to my family."

Aiden knelt beside the woman. "I'm watching this guy's every move. He's the best in the business, especially at such a young age. We need more men like Dr. Drew."

Jace took out a notebook. "Do we have an identification?"

"Rose Penny. Found her driver's license in her pocket." Dr. Drew handed it to Jace. "Guess the killer wanted us to identify her quickly."

"That's odd." Jace read the license. "What can you tell us about the victim?"

"Same MO as the others," Aiden said. "Female in her late twenties. Dark hair. Death by asphyxiation."

Dr. Drew scowled. "Aiden, remember what I taught you."

The younger coroner snapped his fingers. "Right. You'd think I'd get it right after two years. We'll know more after we get her to the morgue, but it appears she was strangled."

Dr. Drew winked at Scarlet. "That's better."

A chill danced across Scarlet's arms despite the warm summer day. She took a step backward as if trying to distance herself from the flirty doctor.

Jace squeezed her hand and released it quickly. Had he sensed her sudden anxious mood?

"Dr. Drew, any suggestions why CLS leaves a string of seashells around the victim's neck?" Jace crept forward. "Seems odd to me."

"And why leave them on the beach—a place most would call peaceful?" Scarlet asked.

The chief coroner's eyes narrowed. "Who knows what this maniac is thinking? My guess is the seashells are to comfort them as they pass."

Aiden moved beside his comrade. "We don't

like to speculate, Constable. However, that's the only reason we could come up with."

Scarlet stepped closer to the woman and inspected the seashells strung together by a crafter's leather cord. She knelt to get a better look. All the shells were meticulously spread apart. "Look at this. See how the shells are spaced evenly?"

"Yes, they all have been," Aiden said. "Why?"

"This tells me CLS strangled her and placed the necklace on after, ensuring each shell was the same distance apart. Odd." Scarlet stared at the rest of the woman's face. "Wait. Did all the others have this shade of bright red lipstick on?"

Jace circled around the woman's body. "No. The rest had bare lips. CLS is changing it up. Why?"

Scarlet rose. "He…or she…is evolving."

"Coming into their own," Dr. Drew said. "Is that natural with serial killers?"

"Olive might be able to tell us." Jace made a note on his coiled pad. "Gentlemen, anything different with this victim?"

"Nothing. We'll know more once we examine her more closely." Dr. Drew snapped his medical bag closed.

"Any way to determine the shade and brand of the lipstick, Doc?" Jace asked.

"Not sure. I'll get back to you." Dr. Drew stepped away from the body. "Constable Allen,

I assume your team has finished their initial examination of the scene?"

"Yes." Jace flipped a page in his book. "Can you give us a minute? I want to take a closer look."

Dr. Drew nodded.

"Jace, I'm going to talk to some of these witnesses. See if they saw anything suspicious. Then diagram the scene." Scarlet pointed to a driftwood log beside the body. "I'll be there."

"Sounds good."

Scarlet approached a group of onlookers and asked if anyone had seen anything. She explained she only wanted a description to help draw for identification.

They shook their heads.

Either CLS had placed the body when the beach was vacant or these individuals refused to get involved. Either was possible.

She thanked them and moved to the log, brushing sand from it before sitting. She opened her portfolio bag and removed her tablet. After swiping the screen, she selected the diagramming program and fiddled with the buttons. Thankfully, she'd researched a bit to refresh her mind on how to use it. She surveyed the beach and the angle where the victim's body lay.

The woman's feet pointed to the sky, perfectly straight. If she had struggled, wouldn't they be in a different position? The killer had thought of everything, telling Scarlet they had meticulously arranged the body. From her praying hands to her even, neat feet. Why?

Wait. She jumped up and circled the woman. The body was also void of any sand. "Jace, this killer is particular in every action. Every placement of their victims. Did you notice there's no sand on her body? How is that possible on a beach, especially if she fought back?"

"Good observation. CLS took time to brush sand off and position her, or—"

"She wasn't killed here," Scarlet said, finishing his sentence.

"Right." He turned to the coroners. "Have you any indication the body was moved? Have all victims been cleaned?"

Scarlet snapped her fingers. "Wait, that's not right." She flipped open her notebook. "I wrote in my notes that Lila stated she was on the beach when she was strangled, so she wasn't moved. Plus, she heard someone else nearby. Why would CLS kill one victim somewhere else and not the other? Makes little sense."

"Constable Wells, nothing about this killer makes sense," Aiden said.

More questions. Not enough answers. They required a lead. Something to give them a break in the case.

Scarlet sat on the log again and clicked her program. She studied the body but this time included the crime scene's circumference. She wanted to add everything—sand, driftwood, body of water.

She chose the appropriate template and added the details. She would include the constables' photos once she downloaded them.

Jace walked over. "How's it going?"

"Coming slowly. I need to take a short walk. Clear my head." She stood. "If that's possible."

"Stay close, so I can see you. I'm praying." He moved back to where the coroners were finishing their initial assessment.

Scarlet strolled to the shoreline and stared at the horizon. Clouds rolled in, covering the sun and giving relief from the already intense mugginess filling the air. A sailboat bobbed in the water, picking up speed in the current.

Did she believe prayer helped?

Not even that small memory returned.

Lord, if You're real, help me remember. Help me draw. Anything.

She took off her shoes and socks and walked down the beach, letting the sand and water flow through her toes. The breeze flailed her hair in every direction. She'd forgotten to put it in a bun earlier but didn't care. The sensation of sand, warm water and the gentle wind brought a rush of peace. She stopped and breathed deeply.

Was this an answer to prayer or a quick flash

of memory from time spent at her grandparents' home?

She'd take it either way.

You can do this, Scarlet.

Determination straightened her shoulders, and she returned to the log. She wanted to draw the scene along with the diagramming. A half hour later, a sketch emerged on her paper.

The woman's body, the seashell necklace, Jace and the coroners surrounding the scene. As well as the bystanders, still watching from the sidelines.

She leapt to her feet and walked over to Jace. "I did it!"

The coroners zipped the body bag and lifted it onto a gurney before heading to their van.

"Did what?" Jace asked.

She held up the sketch pad. "I drew. It's only a rough crime scene sketch, though. No memory returned."

"It's a start." Jace rubbed her shoulder. "Listen, Carter tasked me to foot patrol for the rest of the day. I thought you could come and meet the locals. Maybe get some leads."

He really didn't want her out of his sight.

She shrugged. "Sounds good. I might learn something from your years of service on the police force."

He smirked.

Their cell phones sounded a social media alert.

Scarlet looked at the screen.

Pictures of the task force, her sketching from the log and the woman's body were posted with a caption.

See how close I can get? CLS is always watching.

Tension entwined every muscle in her body, robbing her of strength and courage.

SIX

Jace read the angst on Scarlet's contorted face. He took her by the arm to prevent her collapsing and bit back his anger at himself for allowing her into the field so soon after being discharged. He had pressured her too much, but he needed to do his job and keep her safe. It was the only way to do both. She required rest. "I'm taking you to the cottage. I've pushed you too hard."

"I'm good. This alert took me by surprise. That's all." Scarlet motioned toward the group gathered under a nearby tree. "I talked to the crowd, but no one saw anything."

Jace swiped through the pictures on his cell phone. "How did CLS get so close?"

Scarlet leaned over his shoulder and peered at the photos. "Most cells have good cameras."

Jace ignored what her presence did to him and zoomed in on the pictures, studying them one by one. "Wow. These photos prove the killer is watching us." His face heated at the thought of how close CLS had been to them and, more specifically—to Scarlet.

She gulped audibly. "Is CLS still here?" She scanned the onlookers.

Jace's cell phone buzzed. "Carter calling, probably in reaction to the social media post." He punched Answer and the speaker icon. "Chief. I'm here with Scarlet. What's up?"

"How is CLS taking photos of our team at the crime scene now?"

"Perhaps he or she is getting bolder about taunting us."

"And that's when they'll mess up. The mayor is breathing down my neck, Allen. Find answers. Now." Carter didn't wait for a response but ended the call.

"Is he always that forceful?" Scarlet tucked her pencil next to her sketch pad and closed the portfolio bag.

"Yup. But to be fair, I don't think he's ever seen crime this horrific in our Coral Bay area. We're known as a peaceful community." He paused. "At least, I haven't, and I've been on this force for a few years now."

Scarlet's cell phone dinged, and she read the screen. "Olive. Her boss approved her working the case, and she now has all the files."

"How long before she can provide a profile?"

"I'll ask." Scarlet keyed in a message. "So what's the game plan for the rest of the day?"

Jace checked his watch. "We'll grab lunch and head downtown to talk to the locals. You'd be surprised at how much information we get from them."

Her phone dinged again. "Olive says tomorrow. She'll work on it all day and night. Her leader's orders."

"He knows the importance of the case. CLS is getting national coverage." Jace stuffed his notebook into his short-sleeved uniform shirt pocket and looked at the sky. The clouds had darkened, and a fog hovered. "Let's go before this weather turns nasty."

Forty-five minutes later, Jace led Scarlet into Coral Bay's downtown district. As usual, the main street bustled. It was a favorite tourism spot, and the locals basked in the attention.

"Wow, it's beautiful here." Scarlet hung her portfolio bag strap over her shoulder and exited the cruiser.

Jace stepped out of his vehicle and studied the sky again. "Looks like we may be in for a storm. They roll in quickly around here." He gestured her forward. "Did you know many Christmas movies have been filmed in Coral Bay?"

Scarlet scanned the shops lining the street. "I'm not surprised. It's perfect for romance. You can almost feel it in the air."

Jace laughed. "Except there's a killer on the loose. Not sure how well that would go over with fans."

Scarlet pointed to a wooded area at the end of

the street. "Is that a trail? Right in your downtown?"

"Yup. It's a great place to unwind during the day, but most joggers use it early in the morning or at dusk. I love that it's so close. Gives us a place of solitude from our busy days." He walked toward a small market set up along the street. Various fruits, vegetables and flowers lined the displays. "Area farmers also set up this for local business owners and tourists visiting our town."

She followed him and fingered a bouquet. "Quaint and handy. So, where do we start on our foot patrol duty? Is there a normal route?"

A mail delivery truck parked by the curb.

"We walk the streets, beach areas, etc. Talk to the locals. Making sure nothing is out of place. Help the homeless. That sort of thing. Let's start with the letter carrier." Jace waved him over.

The male postal worker approached the duo. "Hey, Constable Allen. How are you today? Heard some of you got injured in that attack." He turned his gaze to Scarlet. "Well, who is this beauty?"

"Constable Scarlet Wells, this is Ian Miller. One of our letter carriers. Scarlet is helping us on a case here in the area."

Scarlet nodded. "Nice to meet you. How long have you lived in Coral Bay?"

Ian adjusted the mail bag strap across his body. "All my life. Love our tight-knit community. Everyone knows everyone's business."

Scarlet smirked. "Which can also be a bad thing, huh?"

Ian's eyes hardened. "Not in my books. We protect each other."

The man's harsh tone showed a sudden shift in mood. Time to steer the conversation onto the case. "Ian, we're trying to uncover leads on our investigation. Have you seen anything suspicious in your travels delivering mail? Any residents acting unusual? Being secretive?"

Ian's face paled beneath his furrowed brows. "You want me to spy on my friends and neighbors? Not happening. Good day, Constables." He stomped down the street.

Jace whistled. "Wow. He's never been that rude before."

"I guess it's my charming personality." She plunked herself on a bench beside the coffee shop.

He shifted his duty belt and sat. "I believe he's hiding something. I saw fear in his eyes. The question is, what's he scared of?"

Scarlet slumped in her seat. "I wish I could remember CLS's face. We would be farther ahead with a sketch."

"Stop beating yourself up. It's not your fault you were injured."

The coffee shop door flung open, and Taylor exited, juggling a tray of paper cups.

Jace stood. "Taylor, let me get that for you."

"Don't need your help. Bad enough I've been

demoted to bodyguard duties, but now I'm being sent on a coffee run?" Taylor turned to Scarlet. "You remember anything yet or are you faking?"

Ouch. Not only was this constable rude to him, but now Scarlet? "Taylor, what's your problem?"

Her eyes narrowed. "My problem?" She gestured toward Scarlet. "It's her being here."

Scarlet's jaw dropped. "Have I offended you?"

"You have no right to be here on our team."

Jace dug his nails into his palms. "She has every right. She's the best at what she does."

"She's only here because *you* asked for her." Taylor marched to her cruiser, got in and sped down the street.

An ice cream truck drove by, honking its horn to entice children to buy a treat, even though the weather had changed in a flash.

Scarlet's gaze clouded, then followed the vehicle. "Wait, did Gail say you requested me? Have we been in touch since college?"

He couldn't admit he'd kept tabs on her without revealing his crush. "No, we haven't, but once we knew Lila was still alive and could be a potential witness to identify CLS, we discussed bringing in a sketch artist. I remembered an article about how you helped solve a major cold case using your skills."

"Oh, you mean the teenage girls one?"

"You remember?"

Scarlet shifted her stance, her expression once

again turning sad. "No, I searched on my name and found that article."

Jace silently prayed, asking God to bring her memories back. Would He listen? Not only for their case, but also for Scarlet herself. How would it feel to not be able to remember your past? "Let's continue with—"

A woman's distant scream interrupted his statement.

He pivoted in the sound's direction.

"It's coming from the trail. Let's go." Scarlet bolted.

"Wait!" Jace unholstered his weapon and chased after her.

He wouldn't let anything happen to the beautiful constable. Not on his watch.

Tension formed in Scarlet's chest at the sound of the woman's cries, and she tightened her grip on her Smith & Wesson. She rarely used her weapon but was thankful to have it in her hands. Someone's life depended on it. She ran toward the trail in the wailing sound's direction.

She stopped short when she saw the path's sign. *Bull Thistle Trail.* Why did that name sound familiar? She searched the recesses of her faulty mind, but nothing surfaced. Something niggled at her, suggesting whatever she couldn't remember was somehow important.

Somehow life-threatening.

Footsteps approached.

Scarlet whirled around but saw no one. For some odd reason, the path was vacant of joggers.

Ice chilled her spine, and the overwhelming sense of being watched plagued her. Where was Jace? How had they gotten separated? She hadn't waited for him to follow but had assumed he was right behind her.

The scream blared again, from deeper in the woods. It plunged her back to the notes she'd taken of Lila's interview. Was this the trail CLS had abducted her from? She hesitated.

Another cry—this time a weakened scream.

She couldn't wait for Jace. The woman was in trouble and desperately required help. Scarlet raised her weapon and proceeded onto the trail with caution, her portfolio bag digging into her shoulder. She ignored it and advanced. Dense fog covered the thickly wooded path, crowding her, and sent her stomach churning. Fear strangled every ounce of strength from her body, but the screams propelled her forward until she came to a fork in the path. Which way?

The woman's cry answered her question. Scarlet turned right. Movement in the trees drew her attention, but it was too late. A force shoved her to the ground hard, knocking the wind from her and immobilizing her limbs. Her gun clattered onto the path, out of her reach.

A masked individual dressed in a hoodie straddled her, holding her arms down with their knees. They placed a device on the ground. "You should have gone home." The high-pitched, whispered voice prevented her from determining if it was male or female. "Now, you'll pay."

The attacker wrapped their hands around Scarlet's neck, crushing her windpipe.

Her strangled cries squeaked on the abandoned trail. Would this be how she died? Without a memory and alone in the woods? *Lord, help me!* She kicked her feet, trying to get any type of leverage to escape the assailant's deadly grip.

Pounding feet shouted on the path, bringing her hope of rescue.

"Scarlet, where are you?"

Jace. *Thank You, God.*

Scarlet mustered strength and pulled her knee upward, hitting the person in the back.

The masked suspect yelped and rolled off her. Hopping to their feet, the attacker raced into the dense woods, disappearing into the fog.

"Over here!" Scarlet eased herself up, coughing and gasping for breath. She inhaled and exhaled.

The object on the ground caught her attention. A recorder. She took a tissue from her pocket, picked up the device and pressed Play.

A woman's screams sounded.

A ruse to bring her to this trail. Which meant— CLS had been watching and had tried to take her out again. She scampered to her feet, gasping for breath.

Jace appeared beside her. "Don't leave my side again." His nostrils flared.

The tension in his voice told her she'd scared him, but now wasn't the time for regret or apologies. She only wanted them to catch the suspect.

"Masked person just escaped. Tried to strangle me."

"*What?*" He brought her into his arms. "Are you okay?"

"Better now." Her body went limp in his embrace, then she popped back and held up the recorder. "They used this to draw us down the path. Why weren't you right behind me?" Her words came out in wheezing breaths. She rubbed her neck to soothe the pain from the attacker's grip.

"Someone shoved a box of vegetables at me. I fell."

Scarlet drew in a sharp inhale. "The suspect was trying to get me alone." She played the recording again.

"Which way did they come from?"

She pointed toward the woods on the path.

"Let's go!" He raised his sidearm and bolted into the brush.

She picked up her gun, shoved the recorder into her pocket, and followed him. Moments later, they emerged from the trail and into the back alley of the downtown core. Business owners were out gathering their garbage. A cable technician loaded equipment into her truck.

Jace stopped by her. "Kinsley, did you see a masked person run this way?"

The slender brunette shifted her ball cap and tucked her tool belt into the back of the van. "Hey, Jace. I didn't see anyone."

"Odd. They would have gone right by you. Scarlet, this is Kinsley Harrison, cable technician." Jace addressed the other woman. "You've been in many homes with your job. Have you seen anything unusual lately?"

The young woman stepped backward, stumbling into her van. "Why? What have you heard?"

Scarlet and Jace exchanged glances.

The woman's nervousness revealed something she didn't want the officers to find out.

"Nothing. We're investigating a case. What is it, Kinsley? What do you know?" Jace asked. "You can trust us."

"No, I can't. You're cops. I gotta get to work." She climbed into the van and sped away.

"Well, I wonder what that was about." Scarlet twirled a hair strand around her finger. "She clearly knows something and doesn't want to tell us."

Jace surveyed the back streets. "Whoever stalked you is long gone now."

Scarlet massaged her neck. A bruise would no doubt materialize any time. Even though weariness plagued her, she had to press onward. Perhaps caffeine would help. "I'd like a latte. How about a midafternoon break?"

He scrunched his nose. "Latte? No, thanks. But yes, I'll have some tea. Let's go."

Did he know how adorable he was with that expression?

She ignored the feelings creeping up on her and followed him to the front of the shops. Scarlet couldn't let any romantic thoughts sway her away from solving the case and regaining her lost past. Even if the temptation hit her over the head with a proverbial two-by-four.

Scarlet sprinted to catch up to his long strides.

Tires screeching caught her attention.

Scarlet and Jace whirled around.

A black F-150 jumped the curb and pulled onto the sidewalk, careening toward the duo. Her brazen attacker had returned to finish the job. Would CLS's relentless pursuit *ever* end?

Could they escape the driver's deadly path before it was too late?

SEVEN

Jace thrust his arms around Scarlet's waist and propelled them both toward the coffee shop, away from the truck's trajectory. They landed against the weathered door. Hard. The force of their combined bodies burst the glass, sending slivers into their skin. Cuts stung his arms and face, but he ignored the pain. *Lord, protect Scarlet's head from further harm.*

Screams erupted inside the establishment at their sudden appearance. People scrambled from their tables, sending dishes crashing to the hardwood floor.

Jace struggled to stand, forcing strength into his limbs. "You okay?"

"Yes!" she yelled, holding on to a bleeding cut on her arm. "Go get that maniac."

He unholstered his Glock and ran out the broken door, raising his weapon.

The truck had plowed into a fire hydrant, letting loose a water spout that rained down on anyone in its path.

A woman and a teenage boy were sprawled out on the sidewalk. The driver had injured more than their intended target. Jace gripped his weapon tighter. What kind of person would try to run down innocent people?

They both moved, indicating they were alive. *Thank You, Lord.*

Jace hit his radio button. "Officer in need of assistance. Roll an ambulance and backup." He spieled off the address and inched toward the driver's door. "Police. Come out with your hands raised."

The driver stepped on the gas and drove over the curb, speeding down the street.

Jace memorized the license plate.

Scarlet stumbled from the coffee shop. Blood dripped down her arm and face. She swatted it from her eye and scurried to the people on the ground. "Are you hurt?"

Jace holstered his gun. "I've called for an ambulance. Did the truck hit you?"

The young woman rubbed her shin. "Just grazed me, but I hit my kneecap hard on the sidewalk."

"Same here," the wiry-haired teen boy said. "That dude sure was in a hurry."

"It was a man?" Jace asked.

The boy scratched his head. "Not sure. They wore a hoodie. Just assumed a guy."

Scarlet grimaced. "Same person who tried to strangle me."

"They were stalking you." Jace eyed her. "You're bleeding, and now there's a bruise."

Her hand flew to her neck. "I'm fine. Minor wound."

Sirens wailed in the distance and grew louder as they approached. An ambulance and police cruiser parked alongside the curb in front of them.

Chief Constable Carter hopped from the vehicle. "Allen, you guys okay?"

Jace eased into a standing position. "Minor cuts and bruises, but fine. Attacker tried to strangle Scarlet."

The chief cussed.

A male and female paramedic unloaded their medical bags from the vehicle.

Jace waved them over. "This is Maya Oliver and Nathan Ellis."

Nathan knelt beside the woman and the teenager, pulling the strap of his bag off his shoulder. He addressed the boy. "Tell me where you're hurting."

"My knee," the boy said. "Whacked it hard."

Nathan examined both victims.

Maya inspected Jace's cuts, letting her hand linger a little too long. "Your wound may need stitches. Let me clean it up and take a closer look."

Jace winced and pulled his hand back. He despised the woman's flirty attitude. "Check Scarlet first. I'm good. Someone tried to strangle her." He wouldn't let them ignore the constable beside him.

Fifteen minutes later, Maya and Nathan whisked the woman and boy to the hospital. Jace had promised them he and Scarlet would follow to let the doctors look at their injuries closer.

Jace addressed Scarlet. "I need to talk to the chief for a minute. Then we'll go to the hospital."

"Sounds good. I'm going to draw the scene." She sat on the bench and brought out her sketch pad.

He approached Chief Carter. "Can I have a word?"

The older policeman adjusted his hat. "About?"

"Constable Taylor is being rude to Scarlet, and you need to get her to stop. Now." His words came out harsh, but he intended to make his request heard.

Carter pursed his lips. "She didn't like that I tasked her to guard Scarlet."

Jace shoved his hands into his pockets. "I'm tired of Taylor's attitude. We've butted heads ever since she came onto the team. I have no idea what I've done to warrant her wrath, but Scarlet doesn't deserve to be treated this way."

Carter raised his hands in a surrender position. "Don't take your frustration out on me. Taylor has always been jealous of your policing skills. However, she's been going through a rough patch lately. Boyfriend dumped her. Cut her some slack." Carter adjusted his service belt. "Anything you can tell me about the driver?"

Redirection. "No identity or idea whether it was a male or female." Jace snapped his fingers and opened his notepad. "I just remembered. I memorized the license plate. Hard to say if we'll get anything from it. Probably stolen." He jotted it down and passed the paper to Carter.

"I'll run it and let you know."

Scarlet approached and handed the chief the recorder the assailant had dropped. She explained what happened. "Maybe there's something Forensics can get off it."

"Good work. I've got this. Go get checked at the hospital. That's an order." Carter walked into the coffee shop.

Jace prayed the license plate or the recorder would at least give them a lead.

They needed one badly. Not only for the women on Vancouver Island, but for the raven-haired beauty with the lost memories. The fact that CLS had almost gotten to her—on Jace's watch—sent thundered tremors cording his muscles and a thought crashing through his brain.

It was only a matter of time before the Coastline Strangler struck again.

An hour after getting their cuts checked and stitched, Scarlet mustered up every ounce of strength after the multiple attempts on her life and willed her legs to follow Jace into the police station. The chief had tracked down the F-150's owner—Ian Miller, the letter carrier. Police had him in custody, but Ian would only speak to Jace. Scarlet noted her college friend's body language had switched from easygoing to a weakened and agitated state. She guessed the driver's targeted hit had taken more out of him than he admitted.

Plus, Jace had been shocked at the news of Ian being brought in for questioning, as he shared Ian was a gentle-spoken man and normally drove a Dodge. The pieces didn't fit.

However, Scarlet's first impression of Ian contradicted Jace's assessment. The man had been evasive, as if he was hiding important information or protecting someone.

Chief Constable Carter met them outside the interrogation room. "Not sure why he will only talk to you, Allen. Don't disappoint me." The man's stern voice boomed in the corridor as he walked away.

"Oh boy. Something has him riled." Jace twisted the doorknob, and they walked into the room.

The letter carrier fiddled with his ball cap.

After they entered, he dropped the hat like he'd been burned and rubbed his bald head. Odd. What had him so scared?

Scarlet withdrew her sketch pad and leaned against the wall. Drawing the scene had been a natural action for her earlier, so she would try again. Perhaps it would stimulate her mind to remember something. Anything.

Hopefully.

"Jace, I did nothing wrong. Why am I here?" Ian picked up his hat again and stuffed it onto his head.

Jace took out his notepad. "Do you own a black F-150?"

"I do. Just bought it last week. Why?"

"Where were you two hours ago?" Scarlet asked.

"I've been on my mail route." He glared at Scarlet. "All day."

"Then who was driving your truck that almost ran us over downtown and hit innocent bystanders?"

Ian yelped and slouched back in his chair. "The last I checked, my F-150 was at the postal depot, where I switched to my mail truck. If it was used to run you down, someone stole it." He looked away.

Scarlet sketched the man's face. "What aren't you telling us?"

Ian slammed his hand down. "I. Did. Not. Do. This. It's obvious someone is framing me and stole my vehicle to hurt you. Call my boss. He'll confirm I have been working all day."

"We will, but why would someone target you?" Jace keyed on his cell phone. "Have you gotten into something illegal?"

Ian's eyes bulged, and he looked down.

Bingo. Was Jace correct and this man was CLS's helper?

Scarlet drew the man's rigid body, bringing their interrogation to life on paper. "Are you helping CLS?"

"Who?"

"The Coastline Strangler." Jace circled the table. "Ian, CLS is in the news, so there's no way you've never heard of the serial killer who has taken six women's lives. You're keeping something from us. What?"

"They'll find out," the man whispered. "They're watching."

"What are you talking about?" Jace halted and pressed his hands on the table, leaning close to Ian. "We can protect you. Tell me what's going on."

Scarlet noted the shift in Ian's eyes from anxious to forlorn. Something saddened and scared him—or was it someone? She held her breath in anticipation of how he would answer Jace's question.

The letter carrier bit his lip.

The room silenced.

Ian shifted in his chair. "You have to promise—"

The door opened, and a man dressed in a suit

stomped through, slamming his briefcase on the table. He waggled his finger at Ian. "Don't say another word."

Ian flinched at the lawyer's sudden appearance before his gaze moved to Jace, then Scarlet. Sweat beaded his forehead.

The counselor's presence frightened Ian.

Why?

Jace stood beside the man, his nose crinkled in disgust. Jace's six-one frame shrank in comparison to the lawyer's towering stature. "Brody Kellogg. Who called you here? I thought you only represented business clients."

What was this man's story that hardened Jace's expression? Scarlet once again let her pencil fly across the page, sketching Ian's counsel. She wanted to capture everything.

"None of your concern, Constable Allen. Unless you're charging him, I'm taking my client with me." A pause. "Are you?"

Jace retreated and gestured for Ian to follow his lawyer. "You're free to go, but don't leave town. We're not done with you."

Ian hesitated, once again gnawing his lip. He stood slowly but kept his distance. The man's repelled body movements toward his supposed defender revealed more than words.

The overpowering Brody Kellogg scared him and, obviously, the letter carrier didn't want to leave with him.

Jace moved to the doorway. "Ian, remember what we said, okay?"

Brody seized Ian's arm but kept his gaze focused on Jace. "Stay away from my client if you know what's good for you. Or else."

Jace matched the man's stance. "Are you threatening a police officer, Counselor?"

Brody's eyes flashed fire. "Take it how you want." He hauled Ian from the room.

"What was that all about?" Scarlet asked. "You two have a history?"

"You could say that. Went to high school together. He's the mayor's son and has gotten away with everything his entire life." Jace rubbed his forehead. "He assaulted a female classmate, but when I convinced her to charge him, his politician father stepped in and the police backed down. He's never forgotten that, and we butt heads constantly."

"How does this all tie to CLS?" Scarlet closed her sketchbook. "It's obvious Ian is scared about something. What?"

"All good questions." Jace glanced at his watch. "It's the end of my shift, and you need rest after today's events. Let's pick this up tomorrow. Maybe it will make sense then."

Scarlet gathered her portfolio bag and followed Jace from the room.

Chief Carter greeted them in the corridor. "Sorry about Brody. He blindsided me with all his legal mumbo jumbo. Got your text and called Miller's boss. He confirmed Ian checked in with him at the same time as the truck tried to run you down. Also, he walked out to the parking lot. Miller's truck is gone, and there's glass on the pavement."

"Someone stole it. Why didn't anyone hear that?" Jace asked.

"Lots of noise inside a place of business. Printers, mail-sorting machines, air conditioners, people on phones." He turned to Scarlet. "Any recollections of CLS's face?"

Her shoulders slumped, anticipating the man's disappointment. Getting on his good side was vital, and remembering CLS would definitely accomplish the task. "None. I'm sorry."

"I'm confident they will return when you least expect them." The chief's cell phone buzzed, and he checked his screen. "Lewis reporting they found the truck torched outside Coral Bay. Forensics will do a thorough sweep, but it's doubtful they'll find anything. See you both in the morning. 0800 hours. Your sister will give us her profile." He walked away.

"Supper at my place?" Jace asked. "Charlie's been asking for you."

The idea of spending more time with him and his sweet son piqued her interest, but her weary body only wanted rest and solitude tonight. She rubbed her neck. It *had* been a long day. Plus, she wanted to reflect. Perhaps that would help her remember everything she'd forgotten.

She stared into his kind eyes. "Thank you. Would love that, but I need to be alone. Well, as much as I can with Gail hovering. Another time? I hope you understand."

He held her gaze a little longer than normal. "I do. Please know I'm praying for you. God's got this."

Does He? Scarlet wanted to believe in a protector looking out after her, even when she couldn't feel His presence.

After supper and while Gail watched a TV game show, Scarlet made a decaf coffee and wandered through the three-bedroom cottage, hoping the stillness would release memories. She admired the beach lover's theme throughout and took a sip of her butterscotch-flavored coffee. The buttery-nut taste lingered on her tongue. *I could get used to this.*

A Bible sitting on her bedroom's nightstand drew Scarlet's eye. She walked over and picked up the teal leather-bound King James version. A memory flashed—Scarlet as a little girl sitting on her grandmother's knee, listening to her read David and Goliath's story.

She drew in a breath. How could she remember that from so long ago but not recent memories? Perhaps the Bible would help stir further recollections.

Scarlet scooped up a teal-and-beige blanket

and her gun and walked back into the living room area. "You okay if I go outside?"

Gail groaned. "It's not safe."

She waved her weapon. "I have my sidekick. I'll be fine." She opened the patio door.

"Wait! Let me do a sweep first, and I'll sit out with you." Gail exited the cottage.

Great, so much for alone time.

Fifteen minutes later, she stepped onto the patio. The skies had cleared and crickets chirped, matching the twinkling stars. The waves crashed against the shoreline.

Gail perched herself on the patio's wooden railing, leaning against the pole with her weapon by her side and gaze peeled toward the shore. "Listen, I'm sorry about earlier. I was rude. My boyfriend broke up with me recently, and it's put me in a continuous foul mood. I hope you can forgive me."

Scarlet sat in the rocker. "I'm so sorry. I understand. Relationships can be tough."

"That's an understatement. I'll let you read now. I just wanted to get that off my chest."

"Appreciate it." Scarlet stared into the peaceful night and took another sip of coffee. Images of her grandparents helping her dig for clams filled her mind. The sense of a happier time in her life washed over her.

A time she wished she could bottle. *If only—*

She shrugged off the thought and set her coffee beside the lantern on the small table before opening to the Bible's table of contents. Where to start? She ran her finger down the list of books and stopped at Psalms. Why? Did it have meaning in her life? Something about it lured her in. She flipped to the beginning and read.

A branch snapped nearby, jolting her from her peaceful thoughts.

She straightened, and the Bible dropped from her hold, tumbling to the deck.

Scarlet leaned over to pick it up.

A bullet whizzed by her head, crashing into the window behind her.

"Get down!" Gail yelled.

Another shot rang out, thundering in the still night.

Scarlet dived to the patio's floor and flattened her body. Images of the childhood bonfire returned, this time with a vengeance. Screams boomed in her ears as the memory surfaced. Flames engulfed her friend.

Scarlet covered her ears to block out the split-second memory, returning to the present. Another shot rang out, hitting the lamp beside her, plunging them into dusk.

"Shots fired. Send immediate backup," Gail screamed into her radio. She recited the address just as another shot splintered the wooden railing. She yelped and collapsed onto the patio deck.

"Gail!"

The policewoman stilled.

Scarlet lunged toward her, but not before movement to the right caught her attention.

A flash of a red-haired ponytail swaying under a ball cap fluttered in the shadows along the cottage's fence.

Violet?

EIGHT

Jace fumbled to retrieve his cell phone from Charlie's night table. His son had just fallen asleep after another nightmare, and Jace didn't want to wake him. Why had monster dreams plagued him lately? Perhaps Jace's trepidation had rubbed off on the five-year-old.

Jace slipped out of his son's bed and hit the answer button. "Jace here," he whispered, exiting Charlie's room.

"Jace! Someone. Shooting. Gail is hurt. Violet." Scarlet's frantic, jumbled words spoke volumes.

She'd been targeted again and was in danger.

"Slow down. Where are you?" Jace moved quickly down the hall in search of Marcy.

"I hauled Gail into the cottage." Her raspy breaths lessened.

"Shooter still there?"

A crash sailed through the phone, answering his question.

God, why won't You stop this madness? Jace's

trust wavered after each incident. He tightened his grip on the phone and set aside his wishy-washy faith attitude. He must protect Scarlet. "On my way. Stay hidden."

Ten minutes later, after explaining the situation to Marcy, Jace parked beside a police cruiser in the cottage laneway. Constables Heller and Lewis passed by the dining room window. Jace exited his Jeep and ran up the stairs, Glock in hand. He assumed the shooter was long gone, but he wasn't taking any risks.

He swung the door open. "Scarlet?"

"On the deck." Her earlier frantic voice had turned to irritation.

Why were the constables exposing her to more danger out in the open? Jace holstered his weapon and stepped through the patio door, bypassing the shattered glass. "Constables, why isn't she inside? Are you trying to get her shot?"

Ouch. Harsh, Jace. Tone it down.

Heller turned, his eyes glaring in the dining room light's beam. "Don't tell us how to do our job, Allen."

Scarlet folded her arms. "Jace, calm down. I was only showing them where I was sitting when the first shot came in."

"Sorry. You sounded frantic on the phone." Jace moved to inspect the deck.

"I was pinned down. Wouldn't you be?"

He nodded. "Understood. Let's go inside so

you can tell me what happened. Lewis, can you search the property?"

"On it." Lewis shone his flashlight onto the cottage lawn before stepping down the patio stairs.

Heller tugged on his gloves and began combing the area for bullet holes.

Jace followed Scarlet inside. His feet crunched on the broken glass.

Scarlet plunked herself on the couch. "Are you always harsh with your coworkers? You're going to get a name for yourself, like I did." She fingered the Bible on the coffee table. "Something I'm working to change. I don't want to be that person any longer."

What did that mean? He sat opposite her and gathered her hands in his. "I'm sorry. I didn't mean to be. I was concerned about your safety. Where's Gail?"

"Ambulance took her before you arrived."

He eyed the Bible. "Have you been reading?"

She moved away from his grip. "Interesting story. I had just opened to the book of Psalms when something startled me and I dropped the Bible. When I went to retrieve it, that's when the first shot whizzed by my head." Her hand flew to her chest. "You can say the Bible saved my life."

God, isn't that just like You? Sorry for my earlier doubts.

"He was looking out after you." He leaned

back, eyeing the mess by the patio door. His pulse thudded in his head, and he rubbed his temples to ward off a migraine threatening to immobilize him. The overwhelming impulse to protect Scarlet slammed him in the gut. "You'll need to pack your things. You can't stay here now that they found you and Gail is hurt."

She moaned. "Is there a hotel nearby?"

"Not good enough. I have lots of room on my property. You can stay with us. I have state-of-the-art surveillance equipment." When he'd mentioned it, Carter had refused his offer to have Scarlet stay there from the beginning. Said his mansion was too well-known. He'd insisted on finding her a secluded place and that Gail be in charge of her protection. Jace wouldn't take no for an answer now. He texted his boss and told him the game plan. Scarlet needed to be safe, and the only way to do that was to keep her near at all times.

"I don't want to impose."

"You're not, and trust me, Charlie would love having someone else to play with."

Scarlet chuckled. "When you put it that way, how can I resist?"

First, Jace required answers to her attack. "Why did Gail let you sit outside?"

She raised her hands in a stop position. "Don't blame her. I needed fresh air, and besides, she did a full sweep before letting me go out. Plus, she sat on the railing, protecting me."

Jace also remembered how persuasive Scarlet could be. "You mentioned Violet. Tell me exactly what happened."

She explained everything.

"Are you sure it was Violet?" he asked after she finished.

"Not exactly, but I don't know any other red-heads in the area. If it wasn't her, why would someone be trespassing?"

Good question. However, Violet had done nothing remotely criminal in the years he'd known her. In fact, she'd helped with many cases, consulting with their lab in Surrey to identify drugs and poisons in tox screens. Her work as a toxicologist had proven invaluable to them.

But she had changed after her horrific experience.

Scarlet wrapped a blanket around her shoulder, hiding the reddened bruise—remnants of CLS's strong hold. "Plus, we still don't know if CLS is male or female."

"Violet being a killer is a stretch, Scarlet." Jace punched in Violet's number. "It's only nine thirty. Let's settle this right now. I need to know why she was lurking around."

"You two close?"

"Grew up together. Known her all my life." The phone went straight to Violet's voice mail.

"Vi, when you get this message, call me immediately. I don't care what time it is." He disconnected.

"I saw the way she looks at you." Scarlet
twirled a strand of black hair. "She wants to be
more than friends."

He huffed. "Hardly. She's the sister I never
had." *Besides, you're the only woman in my head
right now.* Whoa. Where had that thought come
from? *Remember Rene's betrayal.*

Jace sat and his knee bumped Scarlet's, sending a zing of emotions swirling through his mind.
He got up and walked to the open-concept dining room, distancing himself from the attraction
flowing between them.

Or perhaps it was only one-sided.

Concentrate.

Jace cleared his throat. "Do you remember
anything else?"

"Nothing. Only that…" She stopped.

"What?"

"Just something from my childhood. Not important." She waved her hand in the air, dismiss-
ing the memory.

But he caught her twisted expression before
she stood.

"Are you sure?"

Her dark eyes narrowed. "I'm sure."

Jace sensed a significant story still haunted
her from the past. "You can tell—"

The front door swung open.

Jace's hand reached for his weapon.

Lewis stepped inside and stomped sand from his feet. "Found her on the beach."

"Who?"

"Violet, knocked out. She's conscious now and asking for you. Paramedics are on their way."

"Show me." Jace ran outside, Scarlet at his heels.

They followed Lewis to a stretch of beach near the cottage. Violet sat propped against a log, rubbing her head.

Jace crouched beside her. "Vi, are you hurt?"

Violet sighed but kept her gaze diverted. "I'm okay, Jace. Just ashamed of myself."

"What do you mean, Vi? What happened?" he asked.

"I was spying on Scarlet."

Scarlet dropped in the sand on the other side of his friend. "Why?"

Violet chewed her lip, staring at Jace. "I was jealous because of the attention you were giving her. I'm sorry. I know that's stupid. We're only friends." She paused, rubbing her five-month belly. "I watched the cottage from the gate. Suddenly, I heard shots and ran down the beach. I was going to call 911, but before I could, someone hit me over the head. Just woke up when Constable Lewis found me."

Jace embraced his friend. "I'm so glad you're okay. Paramedics will ensure the baby is fine."

Violet jerked away from his hug. "Jace, I caught a glimpse of the emblem on the assailant's jacket before I blacked out. It was from the post office."

What? Was that why Ian was so evasive with them? Could the mild-mannered postal worker be the Coastline Strangler?

The next morning in Coral Bay PD's situation room, Scarlet fingered the heart pendant around her bruised neck. CLS's finger impressions had changed from red to dark purple. Dreams of the strong hands had tormented her sleep, keeping her tossing and turning throughout the night. As she fiddled with the jewelry, a memory flashed, and she sat upright. Her mother had put the necklace on Scarlet on her birthday…just before she confessed the doctor had diagnosed her with Alzheimer's. Everything had gone downhill after that night. A rush of angst bulldozed Scarlet as she remembered the hardship they went through once their mother began forgetting things. *Mom, is this how you felt when you failed to recognize your loved ones?* Tears threatened to fall, but she swallowed to keep them at bay. Right now, she'd concentrate on the case, especially after yesterday's events.

Gail's injury had been mild, thankfully. The

bullet that hit the railing had sent slivers of wood cutting through her arm. It had been enough to knock her from the railing and hit her head, losing consciousness. She'd been discharged but refused to take time off. Paramedics had taken Violet to the hospital and later released her. She and the baby were fine.

Scarlet had moved into a room in Jace's mansion. She guessed it was so he could monitor her after all the attempts on her life. She didn't mind. His presence brought her joy. Why, she didn't know. Plus, Charlie had been ecstatic when he found out the next morning after she arrived at the breakfast table. He demanded she stay and play with his toys.

However, toys would have to wait. Right now she waited for the chief to get Olive on the screen.

Constable Carter had shared with the team that they'd found no additional evidence on either the recording device they'd discovered or the truck. More dead ends. He'd also reported no drugs had been found in any of the victims.

Olive's pretty face popped up on the enormous TV screen at the front of the room. *Wow, you're beautiful, Olive.* Not that Scarlet hadn't studied her sister's pictures on her phone, but to see Olive's face on the monitor magnified the impact of her looks. Her hair was lighter than Scarlet's raven locks, but they definitely looked similar.

"Can you hear me?" Olive asked.

Chief Carter moved closer. "Loud and clear."

Olive caught Scarlet's gaze and waved, then dropped her hand. Her face flushed with embarrassment.

Perhaps her sister wasn't as confident in herself as Scarlet had heard in her voice over the phone. Why? Did her sister hold past wounds, too? Scarlet set aside the question and opened her sketch pad. Her way of capturing information. At least, the drawings in her sketch pad seemed to prove the pencil and paper felt like home.

"Let's get started," Chief Carter said. "Allen, write Olive's conclusions on the whiteboard."

Jace took a marker from the ledge and positioned himself to jot down the profile. "All set. Go ahead, Olive."

The criminal investigative analyst cleared her throat. "Thank you. I want you to know, I've studied all the files, social media posts, autopsy reports and handwritten notes. Both the one CLS sent to the station and the one sent to Scarlet."

Constable Taylor hurried through the door. "Sorry I'm late."

"Why are you even here, Gail?" the chief asked.

"I won't let a little flesh wound keep me down." She plunked herself beside Scarlet.

"I will forward this profile to you, Chief, but here are my conclusions." Olive shifted her papers. "I analyzed CLS's handwriting. The sharp, angular penmanship leads me to believe the Coastline Strangler is male, probably mid-to late thirties."

"You can tell the gender from the handwriting?" Constable Lewis asked.

"No, not with 100 percent accuracy. Especially in today's world, when most kids are only taught to print. However, this person uses a combination of printing and cursive. This is just a guess. I wish it could be more accurate. Plus, most serial killers are male." She turned over a page. "I also think he drugs his victims because he's probably small in stature. Perhaps his way of overpowering the woman. Just in case she's stronger."

Jace wrote "drugs to overpower, small male" on the board. "But no drugs have been found in the tox screens performed."

Olive leaned closer to the camera. "I'd suggest doing a deeper dive on that, especially since Scarlet noted Lila's words about feeling a bee sting and the wooziness. Sounds like drugs to me. There are more extensive testing options that may find something, even though they're expensive to conduct."

"I'll get Violet working on that, since she's a toxicologist. If CLS is using drugs, she'll find it." Jace put the marker down and keyed a message on his phone.

"Moving on. CLS is shy, especially around women. The fact that he chooses victims with the same hair color and age tells me he's imitating someone who had a negative influence in his life. Mother? Sister? Teacher?" She flipped another page. "CLS is probably from the Coral Bay area, since most of the bodies have been left on beaches near you. His social media posts tell me he's narcissistic. He craves the attention, something he never got as a child. He will inject himself into the investigation and be watching your team closely. That makes him dangerous. Stay alert."

Scarlet perfected Olive's eyes in her sketch. "Why do you think he leaves the women on the beach?"

"Something from his past. Either good or bad."

Gail leaned forward. "Perhaps his way of giving his victims peace, because that's where most people go to relax."

"Could be," Olive said. "Or maybe he hated the beach and feels it's the perfect place to rid himself of the women."

Jace snatched the marker again. "Any ideas on the seashell necklaces?"

She shuffled more papers. "Yes, I was getting to that. In my opinion, the seashells symbolize something comforting from his past. A type of endearment."

"So, his way of giving the victim comfort in their dying breaths?" Jace said.

Olive steepled her fingers. "Exactly. Tells me

he has a soft side. Kind of justification to his sickening killer side. In his eyes, of course."

Scarlet studied the latest victim's picture attached to the board. Her red lips seemed too messy for Rose to have applied it herself. A woman would take more care. "Olive, why did CLS just start putting lipstick on them? Is it normal for a serial killer to change their MO?"

"Yes, good segue. That was my last observation. This change tells me CLS is getting into his groove. Finding his own way, so to speak. He wants to stand out, so in his view, he's improving his MO and signature."

Jace wrote a note on the board and turned to the group. "We need to catch this guy before he evolves more. Who knows what he'll do next?"

Olive typed on her computer. "That ends my profile. I just sent my conclusions to you via email, Chief."

Ray stood. "Thank you, Olive. We appreciate your help at such short notice. If you think of anything else, please contact either Jace or Scarlet immediately."

"Will do. I hope it helps you catch CLS before any other women are taken."

"Us, too. Signing off." The chief hit the end button. "Okay, folks, we'll release this profile in a press conference at 1400 hours outside our station. I want the team present to show a unified front. Allen, can you contact the rest of MCU and get them here?"

"Of course." Jace returned the marker to the whiteboard's ledge.

Scarlet closed her sketch pad and packed everything into her portfolio. Her cell phone chimed. She read the screen. It was her boss texting, asking her to call him with Jace present. He had news pertinent to the case.

"Jace, my boss wants me to call him with you there. Apparently, something to do with CLS. However, not sure what it would be from Whitehorse."

"Interesting." He gestured for her to follow him. "This way."

Jace led her into their lunchroom and closed the door, pointing to the small table. "More private here. Have a seat."

Scarlet placed her cell phone on the surface and hit Sergeant Tobias Xander's number.

"Xander here. Thanks for calling, Scarlet."

"You're on speakerphone with Constable Jace Allen. Jace, this is my leader, Sergeant Xander."

"Nice to meet you," Jace said. "What news do you have on the case?"

Her boss let out a slow exhale. "Not so much the case, but on Scarlet."

Fear ratcheted up and exploded throughout her body, sending her pulse throbbing in her head. What information could her leader possibly have?

Jace leaned forward. "What do you mean, Sergeant?"

"Our detachment was targeted and our system hacked early this morning. Someone got to your personal information."

Scarlet gripped the sides of the table, her knuckles turning white. "Isn't our firewall secure?"

"Normally. Whoever did this knows computers," Xander mumbled. "Scarlet, they know all of your family's addresses. We need to get protection detail on your sister, mother and father."

"How could this have happened, Sarge?" Scarlet's lip quivered.

"No idea. Digital Forensics is investigating. I'll know—"

A text popped up on her cell phone's screen, muting her leader's voice.

Olive is pretty. Just my type. Stay out of this investigation or I'll go visit your sister.

Heat flushed Scarlet, propelling tension into her neck and turning her limbs to jelly.

She had to warn Olive before she became CLS's next victim.

Jace caught the fear in Scarlet's widened eyes after reading CLS's message on her phone. Her sister was in danger. He took Scarlet's hand and squeezed, hoping his touch would reassure her.

He'd not only protect Scarlet but do everything in his power to keep her family safe, too. The threat robbed her of words and put her in a frozen state. "Sergeant, can you keep us apprised on your investigation? We have to run."

"Will do. Scarlet, call your family."

Scarlet's lip quivered. Again.

"I have buddies on the force in the Ottawa area," Jace said. "I'll get them to put a protective detail on Olive and her parents."

"Thank you. Scarlet, I'm not sure if you remember this yet or not, but you've been like a daughter to me since I lost my own. I need you to stay safe."

Scarlet moved her hand back, as if her leader's sentimental words jolted her from the trance. "Thanks, Sarge. Stay in touch."

"Will do." He clicked off.

Scarlet snatched her cell phone. "CLS cannot get to my family. I need to call Olive."

"Wait." Jace fished his phone from his pocket. "Let me call my acquaintance on the police force in your sister's area. Met him a few years ago at a bomb training seminar." He scrolled through his contacts and selected the number.

"Zac Turner here," the deep voice said.

"Zac, buddy. It's Jace Allen."

"Hey, long time, no hear. How's it going there in Coral Bay?" A dog barked in the background. "Ziva says hi."

Jace chuckled. "She doesn't sound like a puppy any longer. Listen, I need your help in protecting a family in your jurisdiction."

"Sure, I'll see what I can do."

Jace motioned for Scarlet to sit. "I'm here with Scarlet Wells. Her sister—"

"Scarlet, is something wrong with Olive?"

Scarlet inhaled sharply. "How do you know my sister, Zac?"

Silence.

"Zac, you there?" Jace asked.

"I don't understand, Scarlet. Olive and I were engaged. How could you not remember that?"

Jace slouched back in his chair. "I need to bring you up to speed." He explained about CLS, Scarlet's amnesia and the threat on her family.

Zac whistled. "Wow. Olive obviously hasn't reminded you of our broken engagement. She's stubborn and probably won't want my help, but I will ensure she and your parents are safe. You have my word." Ziva barked. "And Ziva's."

Scarlet smiled. "I appreciate that, Zac."

"Jace, I'll text you once I have their detail in place. Stay safe, you two."

"Thanks." Jace disconnected. "Wow. That was another God thing."

Scarlet wound a clump of hair around her finger. "What are the odds?"

"The law enforcement community reaches far and wide. I wonder why Zac and Olive broke up?"

"No idea." Scarlet stood. "I need to tell her before he shows up on her doorstep."

"I'll advise the rest of the MCU team about the press conference and get you a new phone number so CLS can't contact you further. You call Olive and I'll be back." Jace exited the lunchroom.

Three hours later, Jace positioned himself in the parking lot to the right of Chief Constable Carter in front of Coral Bay's police and fire departments, with the entire Vancouver Island major crimes task force, including firefighters, showing a united front. They meant business. The Coastline Strangler would not evade them any longer.

A crowd gathered on the grass and lined the street. The group standing in front of them proved the residents of Coral Bay wanted answers. The community was scared now that CLS had taken more women's lives.

Scarlet sat off to the right, sketch pad and pencil in hand. Said she wanted to draw as many spectators as she could in the short time the conference would last.

Reporters raised their recording devices as they spaced themselves over the small property's lawn. CB News crew had a cameraman in the center of everyone.

Jace scanned the crowd for suspicious activity. He brought out his notebook and wrote names of familiar faces. Anything to help with the investigation.

Chief Carter stood on the wooden stage and tapped the microphone they'd attached to the podium. "Thank you for coming. As head of the Vancouver Island major crimes task force, we wanted to present you with the profile of the Coastline Strangler. It's time to put CLS behind bars and protect the women from our area." He pointed to the camera. "But we need your help to do it. This killer has taken six women's lives from different parts of our beautiful island. It's time to stop him in his tracks."

"You said *him*. CLS is a male?" a reporter asked.

The chief lifted his right hand. "We don't know with 100 percent certainty, but we believe the Coastline Strangler is a male in his mid-to late thirties. Small in stature. He drugs his victims to get the upper hand." He peered closer into the camera. "That tells me he's weak. He probably had a tough childhood and is from the Coral Bay area. Maybe a domineering mother or sister. He's someone who blends in—shy, quiet, organized, meticulous. Focuses on the details. Someone you probably wouldn't suspect. If you know of anyone who fits that description, we've set up a tip line. Please call this number." He recited the phone number slowly.

The crowd murmured among themselves.

A sudden wind rustled the leaves. Jace peered at the sky. Darkened clouds moved in, blocking the sun's rays. A storm would erupt at any moment.

Chief Carter raised his index finger. "One more thing. We have reason to believe someone witnessed the strangulation of Lila Canfield a few days ago. If that someone is you, please come forward. We need your help." He paused for effect. "Questions?"

A spindly, balding reporter raised his hand. "Why did it take you this long to offer CLS's profile?"

Jace stiffened. The chief must tread carefully. A correct answer to the question was essential. After all, Coral Bay PD didn't need a lawsuit on their hands.

Chief Carter tapped his thumb on the podium. "Time lag in victims. Our suspect killed two women on the other side of the island a year ago. We didn't have enough connections to determine their deaths were caused by the same person."

Jace noticed his leader left out details of the seashell necklaces. They wanted to keep CLS's signature from the public for now.

"Something triggered the suspect to make him kill again, as a third victim was found on Lark Bay Beach right here in Coral Bay two weeks ago. We took a closer look and determined the women all were around the same age, with the same hair color." The chief gestured toward his team. "Then we formed a task force. The fourth and fifth victims were four days apart. However, we lost a member to a targeted hit three days ago—our behavioral analyst. We had to find a suitable replacement in order to provide you with a strong profile. We don't want mistakes in this investigation."

A solid answer.

"So, CLS has accelerated his kills?" another reporter said.

Carter inserted each hand into both sides of his vest. His normal thinking stance. "Seems so. That's why we need the public's help. Please, if you know anything, call the tip line."

A gust of wind knocked Jace's notebook out of his hand. He bent over to grab it.

A blinking red light under the podium caught his eye. Beside it, a digital clock read 0:05.

That only meant one thing.

He bolted upright and pointed at his chief. "Bomb. Everyone get down!"

He lunged toward Scarlet and tugged her to the ground.

An explosion boomed, catapulting his chief into the air.

Chaotic screams ended the press conference.

NINE

Muffled screams turned into distant echoes in Scarlet's ringing ears. Debris from the roughly constructed stage rained down upon them. Jace's weight smothered her, and she struggled to breathe. Pain shot through her arm, throbbing from the twisted impact to the pavement when Jace tackled her. Thankfully, she had been sitting. "Can't. Breathe." The surrounding commotion drowned out her raspy words.

Jace rolled off and brought her into a seated position in the parking lot. "You hurt?"

She clutched her right arm. "Landed on my elbow, but it will be fine. Could have been worse."

Blood trickled down his handsome face like infected teardrops. She rubbed it off and cupped his cheek with her hand. "You're bleeding."

"I'm fine." Jace pushed himself to his feet.

Pounding footsteps thundered in every direction. The crowd was dispersing, and they needed to act quickly. Check for injuries. She scrambled to her feet. Her knees buckled, and she latched onto Jace to steady herself.

"Chief!" Gail screamed.

Scarlet turned in the constable's direction.

Chief Constable Ray Carter lay motionless in the station's doorway. He'd been thrown in the blast.

Jace limped toward his fallen chief.

She followed, praying the man was still alive.

Jace moved Gail aside and searched for a pulse.

Scarlet held her breath.

Jace's shoulders slumped. "He's gone."

Gail sobbed.

Despite the woman's earlier harsh attitude, Scarlet embraced the cop. "I'm so sorry."

Gail's cries subsided. "How did we miss the bomb, Jace? Who had time to place it there when we only set up the stage a couple of hours ago? Police and firefighters have been in and out all day."

Jace's contorted face expressed the same question. The same loss. "Not sure. We'll check the camera footage." His shaky voice revealed his sorrow at losing his leader. "Gail, call Dr. Drew and the paramedics. We'll assess the scene."

The policewoman stared at her fallen boss, frozen in time.

Jace snapped his fingers in front of her face. "Gail. Move. There'll be time for grieving later." His jaw dropped. "I'm sorry, I don't mean to sound harsh, but the chief would want us to protect the others first."

Gail nodded. "On it." She sprinted away, yelling for help.

Scarlet grazed Jace's hand. "I'm so sorry. What can I do?"

His muscles tensed at her touch.

She dropped her hand.

His normally gentle countenance had washed from his contorted face. This violent crime had shaken him to the core.

Of that she was certain.

Even through all of Ray's harshness, Jace had respected and loved his leader.

Sirens pierced the daylight hours, gaining strength the closer they got to the station. A bystander must have already called 911. Then again, Coral Bay was a small, close-knit community. Residents looked out for each other.

Scarlet gazed into the crowd moving about, a question arising. Would any of these locals come forward if they had information about the Coastline Strangler? Or, for some unknown reason, would they protect one of their own?

She prayed that wasn't so. Surely this act of violence would encourage them to share information.

"First, check for injuries." Jace's hardened tone revealed his angst. "Then we will inspect the bomb fragments. Hopefully we'll find something in them that will lead us to who did this." He wrung his hands together. "CLS will pay for this."

A question formed in Scarlet's mind. "Why not set the explosion before the chief had the chance to share the profile? Makes little sense to me."

"I don't know. Perhaps he enjoys being dramatic or feels we'll never catch him. Check on the others. We'll compare notes later."

Hours later, after all the injured who warranted a doctor's care were transported to the hospital, Scarlet eyed the officers combing the area for evidence.

Jace rummaged through a pile of wooden pieces, probably hoping to find something—anything—to convict the person responsible.

She remembered the forlorn look on his face as Dr. Drew zipped Chief Constable Ray Carter's body bag and wheeled it away. It would be a while before Jace recovered from his loss, but for now he concentrated on getting justice for his leader.

Scarlet approached, taking hesitant steps. "Anything salvageable?"

His shoulders tumbled forward in defeat. "Only a few fragments, showing a crudely built homemade pipe bomb with a digital clock attached. Lewis took it to Forensics." He picked up a piece of wood and threw it against the building's brick wall. "Not sure it will help catch the perp."

She squatted beside him and rubbed his upper back. "God's got this, right?" She still wasn't sure she believed that, but he did. Or used to.

Jace rose and stared at the building, now swarming with additional cops and firefighters. Everyone had joined the investigation to right this terrible wrong. "I don't know anymore. Why would He allow this to happen?"

Wow, his faith had been tested by this one act of violence. Or was there more in his life to cause him to question God?

Scarlet stood, the secret her boss had mentioned still eluding her. She could relate. "I don't have the answers, Jace, but don't give up on your faith. Don't let CLS win."

His gaze swung to hers. "You're right. He won't. I'm sorry for being harsh."

"It's okay. I understand. Your chief was a major loss."

Jace let out an audible sigh. "Huge. He could be rough around the edges and pushed me hard, but he was like a father to me."

"Did he have a wife? Children?"

He shook his head. "None. Claimed to be a sworn bachelor. Said he didn't want to put a wife through the agony of a cop's life. You know, the threat of losing our lives on the job. Something police officers do every day they step outside.

Serve and protect." He bit his lip. "However, there were times I suspected he wished for a woman to go home to." His expression changed slightly.

Scarlet studied the lines on Jace's face. Something she sensed she was good at—reading body language. His wrinkled forehead displayed curiosity, perhaps. A thinking stance.

But what are you thinking, Jace?

However, the look disappeared as quickly as it came.

She shrugged her inquiring mind back to the situation at hand. "I hate to ask this so quickly, but who will replace him as leader of the task force?"

"Good question. I'm the senior-ranking officer now that he's gone, but I guess we'll see what the higher-ups decide." Jace rubbed his neck muscles. "Have you remembered anything?"

She shook her head.

"We're losing this battle and need something. Fast."

"Hopefully the tip line will come through for us." Scarlet noticed her discarded sketch pad on the pavement, the pages riffling in the wind as if calling out to her. A thought emerged.

Perhaps she had sketched the Coastline Strangler in her attempt at capturing the onlookers. Her contribution to the case. Maybe, just maybe, it would help trigger her lost memories.

She hustled over, scooped her drawings off the pavement and raised the pad. "This might help. I drew some people from the crowd gathered for the press conference."

She opened the book and stiffened, almost losing her grip on her portfolio.

A rough sketch of a man's face appeared on the page.

Scarlet had started one eye.

She froze. A memory flashed. Her sitting in front of Lila, getting ready to draw the sketch.

And then—an overwhelming feeling of terror sending chills coursing through her veins and turning them to ice.

Her knees buckled.

Jace wrapped his arms around Scarlet's waist, keeping her upright. Her blanched face revealed fear, but from what? A memory? "What is it, Scarlet? Did you remember something?"

"An intense sense of terror." She gulped and raised her sketch pad. "This triggered the memory."

A half-drawn man's eye.

"Do you think you saw CLS here today?" He pointed to the sketch. "And that's him?"

"Possibly." Her gaze darted to the remaining spectators left in the vicinity. "Was he watching today?"

Jace struggled to picture the scene before the

blast, but one thing he knew for sure. "Absolutely. Especially because of his narcissistic personality. He was here."

She waved her book. "But this incomplete drawing doesn't help. It could be anyone."

"Do you remember anything else from Lila's interview?"

"Only that I was sitting in front of her, ready to sketch. The rest is gone." She clutched his arm in a vise grip. "He's watching. I just know it."

"Let's get inside." Jace looked around. "I want to check our camera footage. Maybe we caught CLS on video." He placed his hand in the crook of her back, leading her toward the door.

She trembled beneath his touch. From what?

He snapped his hand away, ignoring the growing spark between them.

There was no room for romance in his life.

Now or ever.

Jace stared at the computer monitor ten minutes later, trying to erase his feelings for Scarlet as he checked the footage from earlier. However, her presence nearby made it hard, especially when her strawberry-vanilla scent wafted into the small room.

An image flashed on the screen, but he missed it.

Concentrate, Jace.

He hit Stop and rewound the footage. Once again, he pressed Play.

A short, masked suspect appeared, dressed in black pants and a black hoodie.

On a hot day. *Definitely our guy.*

Jace leaned closer and paused the frame just as the man glanced in the camera's direction. "Got you!"

Scarlet walked over to him, leaning over his shoulder. "What did you find?"

He pointed. "Does that look like anyone you know?"

She snapped to attention. "That's the suspect who tried to run us down and strangle me. Do you think it's CLS?"

"Has to be. We have no sign yet that he has a partner." He pressed Play. "Let's see what he does."

The masked person tugged his hoodie farther down on his face before pulling a can from his pocket. He edged closer and sprayed the camera, blocking any hopes of them catching when he planted the bomb on video.

Jace banged on his desk. "Figures."

"How did he get by everyone? Was he waiting to see when they finished building the stage? It couldn't have been that easy to bypass everyone coming and going."

Jace grimaced. "This guy is cunning. Thinks like a cop."

"Olive's profile mentions nothing about CLS being in law enforcement."

"Could she have gotten it wrong?"

Scarlet twirled her hair.

He'd figured out it was her thinking pose, or it meant she was angry.

Jace raised his hands in surrender. "We just need to consider he might have either a law enforcement or military background. Remember, he also knows how to handle a gun. He shot at you." His cell phone buzzed, and he unclipped it from his waist. "Hey, Vi. You at home now?"

"Yes. I just wanted to share that I've heard from the lab. We have another tox screen underway."

Jace paced. "How can we ensure nothing is missed this time?"

"I'm not sure what happened at the lab on the other side of the island, but I'm testing for everything. This one will be costly."

"Whatever it takes. I'll pay for it myself if it means catching this lunatic."

A crash boomed through the cell phone, followed by a scream.

Jace stopped pacing, his heartbeat skyrocketing. "Vi! What's going on?"

"He's. In. The. House." Her breathless words revealed her elevated angst.

Scarlet moved to Jace's side. "What's happening?"

"Get my keys. Now!" He pointed to the fob on his desk. "Who, Vi? Where are you?" His erratic pulse matched his frayed nerves.

"Bedroom. He's coming. Help—"

She screamed before the call dropped.

Jace pressed his radio button. "Dispatch, this is Constable Jace Allen of Coral Bay PD. Deploy all available units to this location." He rattled off Vi's home address, just outside the town's limits, before turning to Scarlet. "Come on. CLS's after Vi."

Twenty minutes later, Jace screeched into Violet's driveway and parked behind her sedan. He unbuckled his seat belt and climbed out.

Violet's front door was wide-open.

Jace hauled out his Glock 17. "I can't wait for backup. She's in danger. We're going in hot."

Scarlet nodded and unholstered her Smith & Wesson.

Jace raised his gun and stepped inside Violet's two-level home. "Coral Bay PD. Stand down." Jace's voice boomed from the foyer.

Only the television playing softly in the corner greeted them. A discarded, half-eaten salad sat on the coffee table with a teacup beside it, untouched.

Jace felt the cup. Cold.

A chill inched up his spine like a spider crawling across his skin. Slow and sure.

A distant noise from the second level drew his attention. "Stay right behind me." He tiptoed up the stairs, hugging the wall.

Scarlet followed.

The banging grew louder.

Jace tracked the sound's direction to the master bedroom. He raised his Glock higher and eased open the door.

Violet's cat howled and darted between Jace's legs, scrambling from the room.

His rapid pulse increased tenfold.

A shutter clanged against the open window, but that wasn't what caused his heart rate to spike. Red words written on the wall in lipstick cemented him in his tracks.

I have her. Come and claim sweet Vi.
Catch me if you can, Constable Allen.

A small seashell was sketched beneath the crudely written message.

Jace holstered his weapon and whipped out his cell phone, hitting Constable Lewis's speed-dial number.

Time to get Forensics over to Violet's house. ASAP.

TEN

Scarlet's hard black lead flew across a fresh page of her sketch pad. She wanted to capture everything she could from the crime scene in Violet Kelly's bedroom. It was the only way she knew how to help with the investigation of Jace's childhood friend's abduction. *Every detail matters.* Her breath snagged. Where had that expression come from? Something she, or perhaps a teammate, used to say? She racked her brain, but nothing further came.

She gripped her pencil tighter, her strokes on the paper widening and revealing her frustration over the amnesia plaguing her mind. *Lord, if You're listening, please give me back my stolen past and CLS's face. We need this to end.* She clenched her jaw. Losing her identity sucked the life out of her, and her weary body couldn't take much more.

Jace and his team gathered downstairs, going through plausible scenarios as Forensics dusted for prints. With their permission, she stood in the doorway observing and sketching. The crude message on the wall above Violet's bed surprised them all. Seemed CLS had veered from his normal MO, both with this new act and Violet herself. Even though she fit the age range, she was a redhead. Not the killer's type.

Whatever his *type* truly was.

She finished her sketch and returned downstairs to the group hovering in the cheerful yellow kitchen.

Jace riffled through a box of lipsticks.

Scarlet approached. "Did you find the red one used to write the message?"

"Just a sec." Jace gestured toward the door. "Guys, can you double-check the perimeter for forced entry?"

Constable Lewis scowled. "Bro, you think we missed something the first time?"

"This is my friend, Lewis, and she's pregnant. I need to be sure."

Constables Lewis and Heller exited through the patio door, stepping into the backyard.

Jace rubbed his sinuses. "I didn't mean to sound so bossy."

Scarlet's heart hitched. She'd do anything to comfort the amazing man before her. "You're under stress. I'm sure they'll understand."

"To answer your question, no, we didn't find

the lipstick, but I'm not surprised. I've never seen her wear that bright shade of red. CLS must have brought it with him." He swiped his cell phone's screen and zoomed in on the picture he'd taken. "I wonder why he chose this particular color."

"Is it the same lipstick used on the last woman? Did we ever get the name of it from tests?"

"We did." Jace flipped through his notebook. "Rouge sang d'assassin."

She huffed. "Really? That's French for 'assassin bloodred.' What kind of name is that for a lipstick?"

He held up his hands. "You tell me. I'm not a woman. Why do you think he picked it?"

"Gotta be some significance for him to choose that color."

"Red has a variety of symbolisms. Violence, courage, anger, love."

"Passions." A thought emerged. "Sounds like it could be a special brand. I'll look it up." She entered the name into her cell phone's search engine.

Seconds later, the name and lipstick brand popped up. "Now, that's strange. This color is discontinued and has been for thirty years."

"What? So how did CLS get it?"

"Didn't Olive say in her profile CLS was imitating someone who had a negative influence in his life?"

Jace tapped the kitchen counter. "Yes, a mother, sister or teacher. What are you thinking?"

"Well, since he wouldn't be able to buy it today, could the lipstick have been his mother's? A sister wouldn't be the right age, and I doubt he'd be able to get ahold of a teacher's lipstick."

"So he stole it from his mother to make his victims look more like her, taking his aggression out on them." Jace scribbled a note in his book. "I'm not sure how this helps us find Violet."

"Well, it ties her abduction to the other victims, so we know it's him. The question is, why target Violet?"

"The only thing I can guess is to get to me. He would have seen me standing with the other task force members." He massaged his temples.

"How would he know you're friends?"

"Pretty much everyone knows everyone in a small town."

Scarlet snapped her fingers. "Or…what if he knows she's doing another tox screen, and he's trying to stop her?"

"But how in tarnation would he know that and what's his endgame?" Jace's cell buzzed. He hit Answer and the speaker button. "Did you find something, Lewis?"

"Yes. We're around back." Doug ended the call.

Jace ran through the patio door.

Scarlet followed.

The two constables were positioned beside Violet's bedroom window, staring at the ground.

Had they found a foot imprint?

"What is it?" Jace asked.

Doug pointed. "Almost missed this, since the long grass hid it. Good thing you told us to recheck."

Frank placed a marker in front of a concealed object.

Jace and Scarlet peered closer.

Scarlet stifled a gasp. "Is that what I think it is?"

Jace moved the grass around the object with his gloved hand.

A lipstick tube.

He turned. "You wanna guess it's rouge sang d'assassin?"

No way. Confusion plagued Scarlet. "I don't get it. Why would CLS be so careless as to leave it behind?"

"Maybe he dropped it," Doug said.

"From everything we've learned about him, he's meticulous, so I find that hard to believe." Jace rolled the tube with his finger. "Yup, the same brand."

Frank pushed himself up. "Perhaps something startled him and he had to rush."

"But why is it here by the bedroom window?"

Scarlet tapped her thumb on her leg. "Surely, he wouldn't have taken Violet out through the window. He probably drugged her and left through the front door."

"Doubtful. Too many spying neighbors." Doug retraced his steps and stood at the property's edge, glancing in both directions.

Jace walked toward the constable. "What are you thinking, Lewis?"

"I agree he drugged her, but he took her through the patio door." He pointed to the gate. "He probably parked on the side street that runs into Violet's cul-de-sac, then brought her out the back. He's brazen to do it in broad daylight."

"But how did the lipstick get here?" Frank asked.

Jace caught Scarlet's gaze, his eyes widening the moment a lightbulb went off in her brain.

"It was planted," they both said simultaneously.

Frank folded his arms across his chest. "Why? Why do that, knowing we may get prints off it?"

Scarlet scratched her forehead and stepped closer to the lipstick. "It's a fairly large tube, so we might. I agree, Frank. Nothing about this killer makes sense."

"Lewis and Heller, take pictures of the lipstick and then get it to Forensics. We need to check for prints." Jace massaged his temples. "Something tells me we will."

Jace and Scarlet moved back into the kitchen.

Scarlet picked up her portfolio. "You okay? You rub your temples a lot."

"I suffer from migraines, and one is sitting behind my eyes right now." He reached into his pocket and removed a bottle of prescription medication. "I need to nip it in the bud before it turns into a bad one."

"You get them often?"

He screwed the cap off and set it on the counter. "Enough, but I'm sure the stress of Violet's abduction brought this one on. I'm concerned about the baby."

Scarlet's desire to pull him into a hug of protection overwhelmed her, but she kept the inkling at bay. "We'll find her."

His saddened eyes caught her gaze and held.

Their cell phones dinged, breaking the moment.

Hers played a flute chime.

Scarlet winced. "That's not good. I set that specific sound notification for social media alerts on anything mentioning CLS."

Jace swiped his phone with his opposite hand.

She read her screen.

Pictures of Charlie playing on the beach

popped up on CLS's social media feed, along with a caption.

Constable Allen, see how close CLS can get to you? Stop your investigation or you'll pay.

Jace dropped his bottle of medication, pills clattering to the floor and rolling in every direction.

Scarlet's erratic heartbeat vibrated in her ears. "We need to get to Charlie. Now."

Jace swallowed the lump in his throat, hitting the siren and lights on his police cruiser before squealing from Violet's driveway. *Lord, protect my boy!* He couldn't lose his ray of sunshine. Jace selected his home number from the Bluetooth and waited as it rang. "Come on, Marcy. Pick up." Jace had already called Dispatch to get constables to his home, pronto.

First Violet. Now Charlie. He banged the steering wheel. CLS would not get to his family. *God, how can I trust You when You keep allowing such heartache?* He ran his hand through his hair, fisting a clump as if that would take his frustrations away. He exhaled an extended sigh and let go of his blond locks. *Concentrate.*

"They might still be on the beach." Scarlet

held up her phone. "Do you think this picture is from today?"

Jace stole a quick glance. "Yes, that's the shirt I put on him this morning. Marcy isn't answering."

"Try her cell phone."

Jace punched off and hit Marcy's number.

She picked up on the first ring. "Jace, did you forget something?"

"Marcy, listen to me closely. Grab Charlie and get in the house. Go to the panic room, then lock down the house like I taught you. I will disengage everything once my team arrives."

He caught Scarlet's raised brow in his peripheral vision but ignored it for now.

"You're scaring me. What's going on?" The tone of Marcy's voice revealed her apprehension.

"I'm on my way and will explain. Do it!" He disconnected and immediately regretted the anger in his voice. His nanny didn't deserve that, but he wanted her to know the severity of the situation.

"You have a panic room? Why?"

How did he explain without exposing his fear? His childhood abduction had plagued him through the years, and once he and Rene had Charlie, Jace had had the room constructed. He would not let his family be taken.

"Long story." Jace took the right turn onto the beach road too fast.

Scarlet bumped her head on the passenger window. "Oof."

"Sorry." Jace inwardly chastised himself for speeding and putting Scarlet at risk, but he had to get home to protect his son.

"It's okay. I get it. You're worried about sweet Charlie."

If you only knew.

Fears spawned by his childhood abduction slammed into him like a transport truck at full speed. Jace had assumed he'd dealt with the anxiety, but the idea of Charlie being taken or hurt brought it back tenfold.

Sirens exploded behind them, indicating help joined in protecting his family. Jace turned his cruiser into his long driveway and sped toward his home. After what seemed like an eternity, he parked the vehicle in front of the garage and jumped out.

Constable Taylor parked beside him and hopped from her cruiser. "Wait, Jace. Officers on bike patrol are almost here. Let's do this together."

He eyed his coworker. "Why are you here?"

"I'm feeling better, and you need all the help you can get. We're short-staffed, remember? Where are Heller and Lewis?"

"Taking evidence to Forensics," Jace said. "I have them working on Violet's abduction."

Taylor's radio crackled. She pressed the button. "Come again."

"Bike patrol officers just checked in at Allen's location." Whitney often gave them updates on their constables' statuses. "They're coming up the cliff's steps."

"Ask them to check the perimeter for anything suspicious," Taylor said. "Constable Allen and I will secure the house."

"Copy that." Whitney's voice came through their radios, giving the constables Taylor's instructions.

Jace held up his cell phone. "I'm going to disengage the alarm and locks. Taylor, you go through the rear patio entrance. First, let me warn Marcy." He hit her speed dial number.

Marcy answered on the first ring. "You here, Jace?"

"Yes. You and Charlie okay?"

"Charlie's fine. I told him we were going on an adventure. He was quite excited."

Jace smiled at his son's reaction. "Good. The team is moving inside now. Just wanted to let you know. Stay put until I unlock the panic room."

"Will do."

Jace disconnected and hit buttons on his home security program, releasing the exterior locks.

"Wow. You have the best of the best." Scarlet held her gun tight to her chest.

"Can't ever be too safe." He gestured to Taylor. "Let's move."

Taylor circled around the home.

"Stay behind me." Jace motioned for Scarlet to follow. He raised his weapon and rushed toward the front door of his home. His sanctuary.

At least, that's what he'd thought.

Questions on how CLS could get so close to Jace's small section of a private beach tormented him. He prided himself on offering a haven of safety for his son and beloved nanny.

Trust.

The word popped into his mind along with a verse he'd memorized as a child. *Trust in the Lord with all thine heart.*

He'd failed to give God his trust after these senseless killings started. What kind of Christian was he? A phrase his mother used to say emerged.

God knows what He's doing, so we trust. Completely.

He offered a quick prayer, asking for forgiveness, and skulked through the door of his massive home.

Silence greeted him.

Jace and Scarlet's footsteps echoed on the foyer's marble floor, interrupting the stillness.

Seconds later, movement resonated through the kitchen.

Taylor had slipped through the patio door.

His training kicked in, and he cleared the lower-level rooms with Scarlet at his heels.

Taylor met them in the hallway. "Clear. The constables have also confirmed there's no movement on the perimeter. They're making their way into the home to help check all your levels."

Thirty minutes later, Jace approached the panic room. The team had swept through all the rooms in the house, as well as every part of his property. CLS was nowhere to be found. They had checked and double-checked. Jace had to be sure before letting his son out of his sheltered room. He holstered his weapon and turned off the alarm before opening the steel door.

Marcy huddled in the corner with Charlie on her knee. Her bulging eyes and twisted expression told Jace she was in panic mode.

Charlie hopped off her knee and ran to Jace. "Papa!"

Jace lifted and twirled him. "I'm so glad to see you, bud." He squeezed his son tighter. *Thank You, Lord, for keeping Charlie and Marcy safe.*

"We're on an adventure." Charlie giggled and peeked around Jace's shoulder. "Miss Scarlet, you're here, too. Yay!"

She moved forward. "You bet. Wouldn't miss it. You okay?"

He held his tiny thumb in the air. "I A-okay." He squirmed in Jace's arms, so Jace released his son.

Charlie hugged Scarlet's legs. "Will you play with my toys?"

She tousled his curls. "How about later? Daddy and his team have some work to do first."

Marcy exited the panic room. "Charlie, how about we watch television?"

Jace pulled her aside. "You okay? Sorry for the scare, but we had reason to believe you were in danger."

"I thought you'd never let us out. What happened, Jace?"

He fished his cell phone from his pocket and held up the picture of Charlie. "CLS just posted this picture from today. He was watching you, but I don't know how yet."

Marcy let out a cry. "What? Are we safe?"

"My team scoured the property and house. No one is here, but I will be asking for a protective detail to watch over you." Jace squeezed the tears back in order to remain strong for his son's sake. "I can't have anything happen to you."

"Your fears returning?"

Jace had shared with his nanny about the abduction that had left him with undeniable trauma.

"Well, it certainly threw me for a loop. I'm okay now that I see you're both safe."

"I will pray for protection." Marcy walked to Charlie and took his hand. "Let's go, little guy."

Charlie hopped on one foot by her side toward the family room.

Jace chuckled to himself. His son wasn't the least bit fazed by this episode. If only Jace could feel the same.

His cell phone dinged, announcing a text. He swiped the screen. Lewis.

Forensics found a print on the lipstick tube. Ian Miller. Bringing him in now for questioning.

No way. Ian had kidnapped Violet? Why?

ELEVEN

Scarlet sketched the handcuffed Ian Miller's twisted face. His wrists were fastened to a metal bar attached to the table. Was Jace scared the man would flee? His cocky lawyer—Brody Kellogg—sat beside him, arms crossed and knee bouncing. He'd found out about his client's arrest and stomped into the interview five minutes ago, demanding to know why he hadn't been called.

Before leaving his home and heading to the small Coral Bay police station, Jace had ensured Charlie and Marcy were safe. Gail had promised to stay posted in his driveway to keep a close watch on his family. It was the only way he would leave them. Right now, he tapped his pen on the steel table. Scarlet nudged him, hoping he'd catch her reassurance she was there for him and calm his obvious frayed nerves over the threat to Charlie.

Jace cleared his throat and stilled his pen.

"Brody, we have evidence your client was at the scene of an earlier crime."

Brody leaned forward. "Give me details, Constable Allen."

Jace shoved an evidence bag toward them. "Your client's print is on this tube of lipstick left at Violet Kelly's house." His nostrils flared. "Ian, where is Violet?"

Ian's eyes widened. "I have no idea."

Jace stretched his hands out wide, trying to curb his growing frustration with the man. "She reported seeing a post office emblem on her attacker's jacket. Was that you?"

"No! I would never hurt sweet Vi. You know me—I'm not capable of something like this."

Jace opened a folder and read. "I thought I did, Ian. However, your prints are in our system. You were charged with assault."

"That was when I attended university in Vancouver, and it wasn't my fault. I was at a bar and—"

Brody squeezed Ian's shoulder. "Not another word." He turned to Jace. "Is that all the evidence you have?"

"Why were you at Violet's house, Ian?" Jace asked, ignoring the lawyer's question. "There's something you're not telling us. What is it?"

"Nothing. I'm not sure where she is, and I was not at her house." Ian chewed the inside of his mouth.

Scarlet stopped drawing and studied the man. He blinked multiple times, then shifted in his chair.

A scene flashed in her memory. Her interviewing a victim who turned out to be guilty of the crime, not the witness. He'd also reacted the same way when she had asked questions. Did this mean her amnesia was subsiding? It also told her one thing.

Ian was lying.

She leaned closer and whispered in Jace's ear, "Do you mind if I ask a question?"

"Go ahead."

Scarlet stood. "Ian, your body language tells me you're withholding information. You're chewing the inside of your cheek, blinking and fidgeting in your chair. What are you hiding?" She walked around the table and stopped behind him, placing a hand on his shoulder. "A woman's life is at stake here."

He recoiled. "Don't touch me. I have rights."

Scarlet held her hands in the air and walked back to her chair. "Of course you do, but so does Violet Kelly. Are you the Coastline Strangler?"

"What? No!" Once again, he chewed the inside of his mouth.

Brody swatted his client. "Stop. Didn't I teach you not to do that? Remember our conversation. I won't let him get to you."

Scarlet snapped her gaze to Jace's. Was this

lawyer in on whatever Ian was hiding? A line from Lila's interview entered her mind. She inhaled audibly.

"What is it?" Jace asked her.

"Just a sec." Scarlet wanted to see exactly what she'd written, so she moved back to her chair and flipped to her notes in her small spiral-bound book. The question she'd recorded caught her attention: "Did a witness spook CLS?"

She shoved her book closer to Jace and pointed to the question.

His jaw dropped. He turned to Ian and steepled his fingers in front of his chin. "Ian. I need you to be honest with me. Are you the witness who saw CLS strangling a woman on the beach?"

Ian blanched and yanked his hands back, the cuffs clanging against the metal bar.

Brody jumped out of his chair, knocking it over. The crash resonated in the small room.

Bingo.

"You are, aren't you?" Scarlet asked. "That's what you're hiding. You're scared of him."

Brody jerked his finger at Scarlet. "Enough. Unless you're charging my client, we're out of here." He turned to Jace. "Uncuff him. *Now!*"

Jace held up his hands. "Just wait a minute, Brody. We need answers. Women's lives are at stake here. Don't you want us to catch this killer?"

Scarlet held up her notebook. "You witnessed

CLS attacking Lila, and now he's setting you up to take the blame. You don't have Violet. He does, and he somehow put your prints on the lipstick tube to frame you. Am I right?"

Ian looked down, averting his gaze. His actions confirmed Scarlet's thinking.

A question fluttered through her mind. "Ian, do you know who CLS is?"

The letter carrier eyed the exit. "I'm guilty. I took Violet. Please lock me up."

Scarlet's gaze found Jace's.

He shook his head.

Ian feared CLS and definitely knew the killer's identity. He would sacrifice his freedom to stay alive.

Jace unlocked the cuffs. "You *don't* have Violet, do you? You're frightened CLS will kill you, but for some reason, he's keeping you alive. Why?"

Ian rubbed his wrists but remained silent.

"Come on, Ian." Jace moved to the door. "Tell us. We'll protect you."

The man opened his mouth.

Brody hauled Ian from the chair. "Not another word. We're leaving."

Jace opened the door. "If you change your mind, contact me."

The duo left the room.

Scarlet popped to her feet. "He's protecting someone, but why?"

Jace pressed his lips together, frustration showing in his tangled expression. "No idea."

"My question is, if Ian knows who the killer is, why hasn't CLS killed him to hide his identity?"

Jace stilled and took a sharp inhale. "Maybe…" Jace hurried from the room.

"Maybe what?" Scarlet yelled, running after him. She caught up to him just as he was about to exit the station. "What are you thinking?"

"Just a theory." He pushed open the door.

Scarlet followed him outside.

Ian and Brody stood beside the lawyer's Mercedes. Scarlet could tell by their stern body language they were in a heated debate.

Jace ran forward. "Ian. Wait."

Brody pointed at Jace. "I said, *no more questions.*"

"CLS is someone close to you, isn't he?" Jace paused. "A friend? Relative?"

Ian hung his head.

Scarlet silently applauded Jace's intuition. He *was* correct. The letter carrier was close to CLS and didn't want to release his identity. "Ian, who is it? Do you want more women's lives hanging over your head? Tell us!"

Once again, the man opened his mouth. Before he could say anything, his hand flew to his neck, eyes bulging. He collapsed to the pavement and stilled.

Seconds later, Brody also crumpled to the ground.

"No!" Jace unleashed his Glock and crouched.

Scarlet ducked, glancing at Ian.

A small dart protruded from his neck.

Relative or not, CLS had taken out the witness and his lawyer. They'd both known the killer's identity, and he'd silenced them.

"Get down!" Jace pushed Scarlet behind the nearest cruiser and waited for more shots. When none came, he felt both men's pulses. Nothing. He eyed the darts in their necks and grimaced. Jace clicked his radio button, asking for assistance and the coroner's office.

Friend or not—CLS clearly wasn't taking any risks that the letter carrier or his lawyer would expose his identity. Jace guessed the darts contained some type of powerful poison or a lethal dose of a drug.

Constables Heller and Lewis bounded through the station's door, weapons raised. The two flanked both him and Scarlet in protection.

Lewis waved his Glock in different directions. "Where's the suspect?"

Jace eased himself from his squatting position. "I'm guessing he's gone. He accomplished his mission by taking out the intended targets. Can you both spread out and search the area?

Include a wide block radius. We need to ensure the neighborhood is secure."

Heller's eyes narrowed. "Who put you in charge?"

Jace didn't need this man's attitude, not with a killer in the wind and the loss of their leader still fresh on their minds. "Can we please work together on this? That's what Ray would have wanted."

Lewis seized Heller's arm. "He's right. Plus, he has seniority at the moment until a leader is appointed." He turned to Jace. "Whitney needs to see you inside when you have a second."

"About?" Jace asked.

Lewis shrugged. "Not sure. She was tight-lipped about something. Said it was for your ears only." He turned to Heller. "Let's go." The duo left to conduct their search on foot.

Jace speculated about what Whitney had to tell him, but before he could consider it further, the coroner's van sped into the parking lot. Dr. Drew and Aiden Parker climbed out. Aiden circled to the rear doors as Dr. Drew approached the group, medical bag in hand.

Dr. Drew squatted by Ian. "What happened, Constable?"

Jace explained the situation and pointed to the dart. "We're guessing that contains some type of lethal drug or poison. They both dropped instantly. What's your best guess?"

Aiden walked over, pushing a gurney. "Tsk, tsk, Constable. Remember, we don't guess. We let the science do the talking."

Scarlet tilted her head. "Fine, then. Tell us what type of drug or poison *could* cause someone to drop that fast."

"High dosages of strychnine, cyanide, fentanyl...to name a few. We'll know more when the tox reports come back. However, that may take weeks." Dr. Drew opened his bag. "Step away, please, and let us do our jobs."

"Of course," Jace said. "Scarlet, let's search the property together and look for any evidence the assailant may have left behind."

Fifteen minutes later, they returned to the front of the building after coming up empty. As Jace suspected, CLS had left no footprints or proof he'd been on the premises. He'd obviously taken the shot from elsewhere. Jace prayed Lewis and Heller found some leads. Not that he believed God listened to him lately. He'd proven his mistrust in the One he claimed to love. What kind of Christian was he, anyway?

His radio squawked, interrupting his faith battle.

"Allen, we found something," Heller said.

The coroners loaded the bodies into the van and waved before heading out.

Jace nodded and pressed his radio button. "Where?"

"Two blocks down in back of the Sandpiper restaurant. We need you here, stat."

"Will be there ASAP." Jace quickly texted Whitney and told him he'd visit her later. Right now, he had to see what Heller and Lewis found. "Let's go," he said to Scarlet. "I want you to stay close."

Jace and Scarlet ran down the street and stopped where Heller knelt over an item.

Jace approached. "What do you have?" He moved closer.

A dart lay on the ground.

"Why would the killer be so careless?" Scarlet asked.

"Good question." Jace spied the garbage dumpsters nearby. "Did you check those for any other evidence? A weapon?"

Heller narrowed his eyes. "Lewis is doing that, Allen. We know how to do our jobs."

Jace raised his hands. "Sorry, you're right. I'm just anxious to find Violet and stop this maniac."

Lewis ran toward them, holding a duffel bag. "I found this in the dumpster." He set it down and unzipped it.

Heller stood and gestured to Jace. "Let our higher-seniority coworker do the honors."

Jace didn't miss the sarcasm in Heller's voice. He ignored him, tugged on gloves and peered inside. He whistled before pulling out a rifle. "Here's our weapon."

Lewis pointed to the open side compartment. "CLS was obviously careless. A dart must have fallen out in the process of hiding the rifle."

"He's getting sloppy," Scarlet said. "And that will be his downfall."

"Why use darts and not bullets?" Heller asked.

"Exactly what I was just thinking." Jace opened the rifle's chamber, extracting a dart. He held it up. "Wanna hazard a guess at what's in this?"

"It has to be powerful enough to kill instantly," Lewis said. "What does this say about CLS?"

Scarlet shrugged. "Not sure, but anyone can get information from the internet or the dark web."

"She's right." Jace's cell phone buzzed, and he read the screen. *Unknown caller.* He hit the dismiss button before putting the rifle back in the duffel bag. "Guys, good job on finding this. Can you take it to Forensics? There may be fingerprints on it that will give us a break in CLS's identity."

Not that he really believed that. His gut told him CLS would never slip up by leaving his prints.

Jace's phone buzzed again. *Unknown caller.* Someone was persistent. He clicked Answer. "Jace Allen here."

"Help me!"

Jace sucked in a breath. "Violet? Where are you?" He snapped his fingers to get Heller's attention and put his hand over top of his phone. "See if you can get this call traced." He put Violet on speaker.

Heller nodded and stepped away.

"Looks like an abandoned building. He drugged me, and I just woke up." Her words came out breathless. "Quick, you need to find me. Not sure when he'll return."

Jace motioned for Scarlet to follow, and the pair ran toward the police station. "Who is *he*? CLS?"

"Don't know. He's worn a mask the entire time and hasn't spoken."

Scarlet stopped suddenly, her eyes darting back and forth.

Jace halted just shy of the police station's parking lot. "What is it?"

"A memory," Scarlet said, winded. "Lila said the same thing in my interview. The person who tried to kill her didn't speak."

Did that mean her memories were returning?

A church bell clanged through the phone.

Violet's sharp breath resonated through his phone's speaker.

"Are you near a church?" Jace asked, searching his brain to figure out where all the churches were in the vicinity, especially those that still had a bell. Probably dozens in and around Coral Bay.

"I might be *in* a church," Violet whispered. "The clang was extremely loud. Hurry. He's coming."

"Leave the phone on. We'll find you." Jace bolted toward his cruiser.

A commotion sailed through the airways, but Violet remained on the line.

They had to find her before CLS discovered she'd called them, and heaven forbid—

Jace refused to take his morbid thought any farther. *Lord, keep Violet and her baby safe.*

Scarlet clung to the armrest in Jace's cruiser as he took a sharp right turn onto a highway that hopefully would take them to where CLS was holding Violet. His clenched jaw revealed his angst over his friend's perilous situation. She didn't blame him. They must find her before CLS discovered she had called them. One thought plagued Scarlet—how did Violet get a cell phone? There's no way the meticulous serial killer would not have confiscated any device capable of reaching out for help.

Jace banged the steering wheel. "What do you mean, you lost the signal?"

"Don't shoot the messenger." Whitney's shaky voice came through the Bluetooth. "I was told the call dropped, but they narrowed down the location. You're heading in the right direction. Just a sec." A commotion sounded through the phone. "Gail just told me there's an abandoned church about twenty minutes from Coral Bay."

"That's gotta be Bay Bible Chapel. I know

where that church is located. We've caught many teens spray-painting the outside surfaces." Jace turned his police Charger onto a secondary highway. "Send all available units."

"Copy that," Whitney said. "Stay safe."

The vein in Jace's neck protruded.

Time to calm him down before he took any unnecessary risks. Scarlet squeezed his shoulder. "Jace, we'll find her."

"I hope so."

Fifteen minutes after flying around the curvy landscape, Jace drove into the dilapidated church's overgrown, weed-infested parking lot. The midday sun shone through the holes in the exterior walls. Graffiti splattered the sides. The tarnished bell stood proudly under the rickety steeple.

Scarlet's breath hitched. "This place looks like it could collapse at any minute. We need to get her out, but shouldn't we wait for backup?"

"We can't. Who knows how long before CLS comes back or this building gives out?" Jace turned off the ignition. "Let's go."

They sprinted toward the structure and up the chipped stone steps.

Jace unholstered his weapon and turned. "Ready?"

Scarlet cringed and lifted her Smith & Wesson. "Go."

Jace yanked on the door, and it creaked in annoyance.

They stepped inside and immediately stood in the church's sanctuary. Rotten wooden pews lined the small room, with a broken altar at the front. Beside it, someone had piled boxes to the ceiling.

A rat scurried by them before scrambling through a hole in the floorboard.

Scarlet shuddered at the rodent sighting and asked herself what else they'd find lurking in the run-down church. She tugged Jace back. "Be careful where you step. Something tells me the wood in this rickety place will not hold for long."

He pointed. "Stay close to the side walls. We'll edge our way to the front of the sanctuary and check each row for Violet."

Scarlet took slow baby steps while Jace went down the opposite side. Together, they searched up and down the pews. Scarlet surmised they wouldn't find Violet in the sanctuary. It was too open. She spied a broken door at the front. "Where do you think that leads?" She pointed.

"Basement? She has to be there." Jace moved toward it, a floorboard creaking.

Scarlet inched closer, and they both reached the entrance at the same time.

Jace tugged on the half-broken door. The hinges collapsed, and it fell away, clattering to the floor.

"So much for stealth mode." Jace stepped through.

Scarlet followed.

Jace unhooked his Maglite from his belt and turned it on, illuminating the damaged wooden steps. "Violet? Are you down there?"

A muffled cry sounded somewhere below them.

Scarlet moved closer. "These steps are dangerous."

"Stay here."

"Are you kidding? Alone in a spooky, abandoned church? I'll take the risk and stay with you."

"Tiptoe on the outside right, hugging the wall." Jace gingerly placed his boot on the first step and pushed down, testing before stepping.

It creaked but held.

They crept their way down, treading lightly on every other step, reaching the bottom of the murky stairwell.

Jace advanced deeper into the darkness, his beam their only source of light.

Rusted tables and chairs were stacked against the main room's cement walls. A corridor off to the right led deeper into the pitch-black cellar. Another hall snaked to the left.

Scarlet shivered, not only from the coolness but from the eerie atmosphere. No way was she headed any farther into the dungeon's depths.

Jace turned the light in the opposite direction. "Violet, where are you?"

Scarlet followed, staying close behind him. A dingy, musty smell overpowered the basement.

"Over here," she yelled.

He shone the beam and stopped on Violet, zip-tied to a decrepit radiator, the whites of her terror-stricken eyes revealing her shaken state.

Jace ran to her side. "We're here, my friend. We found you." He withdrew his multitool and cut her ties.

Scarlet stooped down beside the pair. "Are you okay?"

Violet rubbed her wrists and nodded. "Better now that you're here."

Jace helped her to her feet and embraced the redhead. "Has CLS returned?"

Scarlet flinched. Why did the simple hug irritate her? *You know why.* Being around Jace sparked emotions in her, and she speculated they'd had some type of connection in their college years together. She set the thought aside. *Focus, Scarlet.*

"No, I heard a sound earlier, but it must have been rats or something."

"There are definitely those in this creepy place." Scarlet had never thought she'd call a church creepy. After all, wasn't it supposed to be a place where one took shelter? Certainly not where someone would be held hostage.

Scarlet spied the phone sitting next to the radiator, her earlier question nagging at her. "Violet, where did you get the cell phone? Is it yours?"

"It was lodged in a floor crack," Violet said. "I assumed CLS dropped it."

Scarlet looked around the basement. Everything lay broken all over the room. A memory of the clanging bell emerged. Wait—how would the bell be functional in the dilapidated building?

Scarlet walked away from the duo and searched around. "Jace, something isn't right here. CLS just happens to drop a phone and a bell rings in a church that's been abandoned for years?"

Jace drew in a sharp breath. "It's a trap! Let's go." He shoved them toward the exit.

Footsteps shuffling above them stopped any further conversations. Scarlet paused, listening intently.

An item clanged down the stairs.

Jace shone the flashlight beam toward the noise.

A grenade bounced on the last step and rolled in front of them.

Scarlet's body silenced, threatening to immobilize even though her mind told her to flee.

Jace snatched the device and chucked it down the corridor, all in one motion. He pushed them in the opposite direction. "Get behind the concrete wall!"

The trio scrambled to get away from the grenade's trajectory.

The explosion rocked the basement.

Scarlet shielded her head and waited before peeking around the corner. The blast had crumbled the stairs and blocked their only means of escape.

A strange odor filled the room.

Rotten eggs.

CLS had lured them to Violet and the church's dungeon to eliminate them.

Once and for all.

TWELVE

Jace's heart hammered as his breathing constricted. The undeniable sulfur smell told him not only had CLS trapped them in the basement, he'd triggered a gas leak. Jace shone his flashlight around. Smoke and dust caught in the light's beam, revealing the grenade's aftereffects. Thankfully, the explosion had been contained to the other hallway. However, it had caused the stairs to cave in, along with plaster from the walls, blocking their exit. Jace realized a little too late that CLS had used Violet to lure him and Scarlet to this location to take them all out. How had he known Violet was such a close friend? Olive's profile flashed in his mind.

CLS is probably from the Coral Bay area, since most of the bodies have been left on beaches near you.

The Coastline Strangler was obviously someone who knew the police department well. Could CLS be one of their own? Jace cringed at the thought. Then again, small towns were famous for everyone knowing everyone's business.

The picture of Charlie on social media popped into his head. *My boy may be next.* If CLS had used Violet to get to him, what was stopping him from kidnapping Charlie? Childhood abduction fears froze Jace in his tracks. The dust from the explosion stilled, like in a time warp, particles floating in suspended motion. His heartbeat slowed while his pulse thumped in his eardrums.

Scarlet brushed dirt off her clothes, thrusting him back to reality.

It was essential Jace get out of this black dungeon, not only for his son's sake but their own lives. It wouldn't be long before the gas overpowered them all. Then there would be no coming back. He fished out his cell phone and unlocked the screen.

No signal.

He hit his radio button. "Constable Jace Allen here. Anyone hearing me?"

Static responded. He tried again. Nothing.

Something was blocking the radio waves. Perhaps they were deeper into the basement's belly than he thought.

Figures.

He turned to Scarlet. "Do you have a signal?"

Scarlet checked hers and shook her head.

Jace lowered his chin to his chest. *Lord, we need a break. Show me how to get these ladies to safety. Give us clear air.* He lifted his gaze. "Be careful how you breathe. Can you find something to cover your face?" Jace tugged out the edge of his shirt, holding it over his mouth and nose. The fabric wouldn't block the gas for long.

A wave of dizziness washed over him, and he stumbled toward the wall, leaning on it to steady himself. He shone the beam toward Scarlet and Violet. They both blinked rapidly. The leak was zapping their energy fast.

"Stay awake. I know it's hard." Jace tried his radio again. "Constable Allen here. Anyone out there?"

Faint sirens sounded in the distance.

"If you can hear me, we're trapped in the church basement. Gas leak."

Fragmented words crackled through the speaker.

Earlier fears from his childhood abduction and being locked in a confined space assaulted him. Years of counseling had only dimmed his terror. *You can do this.* Jace mustered courage and stepped over fallen debris, shining his light. There had to be some other way out.

"We cannot leave in the direction we came. I'll look for another exit." He shuffled down the corridor. It led to a washroom and one other door. His breathing labored. They were running out of time.

He checked the doorknob. Locked.

Lord, I'm weakening. The girls won't last much longer. Give me Your strength.

Jace backed up, took what breath he could through his uniform fabric and charged at the door, kicking with all his might.

The worn wood splintered from the force of impact. Jace stepped over the fallen pieces and into the room.

A ray of light shone through a crack of a boarded-up window.

Hope surged through him. If he removed the planks and broke the glass, they might be able to breathe in fresh air and also crawl out.

Shuffling footsteps sounded in the corridor. "Jace?"

Scarlet had followed.

"In. Here." His broken words were barely audible.

He moved closer and tugged at the boards nailed across their only means of escape. The wood broke and clattered to the floor.

Spots lined Jace's vision as the room spun. Clean air was running out fast in the enclosed basement. How would he break the window in his weakened condition?

"We're here." Scarlet stumbled into the room, hanging on to a fragile Violet. She eased her down onto the floor and moved to assist Jace. "We'll do it together. Ready?"

He nodded and held on to the next plank.

She joined him. "Now."

They tugged in syncopation.

It burst free, revealing a half-broken window. They yanked the other boards until the window was clear from obstruction.

Jace had to break the rest of the glass. They required air, but he felt himself losing the battle. *Lord, help.* Would God hear his plea?

"Stand. Back." Jace held his flashlight as firmly as he could and smashed it into the window. The glass shattered, and a gust of wind blew through. He gulped in the fresh air. *Thank You, Lord.* But was it too late?

He turned to Scarlet. "Bring Violet close—"

Scarlet and Violet lay on the musty floor, succumbed to the gas leak.

Shouts sounded through the broken window.

Jace pressed the radio button one more time. "Jace. Need help. Gas. Basement window." He swayed.

"Copy that," Taylor said. "On our way."

Once again, spots filled his vision as sour bitterness settled at the back of his tongue.

Had CLS succeeded in taking them all out? The question lingered in his mind as he fell into inky blackness.

"Scarlet, can you hear me?" a voice asked.

Scarlet felt a gentle tug on her arm and struggled to open her heavy eyes, finally succeeding.

Pounding hammered her head as her foggy vision cleared. A nurse hovered over her, checking the monitor. "Why does my head feel like it's going to explode?" Scarlet's question came out in a whisper because of her parched throat. "Need water."

The woman lifted a cup from the table and held the straw to Scarlet's lips. "Your headache is from the leak. You inhaled a significant amount of natural gas."

What about Jace? Violet?

Scarlet sat upright. "Where's the constable and other woman I was with? Are they okay?"

"Over here," Jace said. "I have a whopping headache, too, but I'm okay."

The nurse smiled. "He's behind the curtain beside you. Miss Kelly is on the other side. She's still sleeping, but you're all going to be fine. The baby, too. Thank the good Lord the other police officers found you in time."

Scarlet's memory of the situation in the church slowly returned. They'd barely survived the grenade attack when CLS had unleashed a gas leak from somewhere within the building. Jace had found an alternative escape route since the stairs had been obliterated. The nurse was right. *Thank You, God.* He had sheltered them from CLS's devious plan to take all three of them out of the equation. A verse popped into her mind.

For thou hast been a shelter for me, and a strong tower from the enemy.

She failed to recollect where it was found in the Bible, but the verse proved to Scarlet she had some type of faith.

Had it been there all along, or had she wavered with the supposed secret she held? She burrowed her nails into her palms, trying to force her memory. She wanted to move on from this dark pit overtaking her mind. *Lord, please help me to remember. I need to identify CLS.*

Scarlet took another sip of water. "Can you pull the curtain back? I would like to make sure my friend is okay."

Friend? Why did she suddenly want more than friendship? *Focus.*

The nurse moved to the other side of the bed. "Officer, is it okay to do as she asks?"

"Yes," he replied.

The woman removed the barrier between them.

Jace's blue eyes smiled at Scarlet.

Her breath hitched, and she failed to suppress a soft gasp.

The nurse smirked at her and moved over behind Violet's curtain.

Was Scarlet's reaction obvious? She couldn't help it, but the man's gorgeous smile captivated her. "Are you really okay, Jace?"

"I am. You?" He rubbed his head but kept his gaze focused on her.

She nodded, her words evaporating. How

could Jace capture her heart so quickly—and wasn't she supposed to be sworn off men? *Ugh!* She had to stay focused on the case. "Thank you for saving us. Did any of the team see CLS at the church? He must have been there to see us enter."

"I'm waiting to hear from Heller. He's leading the team on a search. They've entered wearing gas masks, but CLS wasn't in the building. Not surprised. He obviously observed from the sidelines."

"Have they found any evidence in the church?"

"Nothing yet. I—" His cell phone rang, interrupting them. He pulled it from his pocket and swiped the screen. "Speaking of him." He punched the button. "Heller, find anything?"

Jace paused, his eyes widening. "Copy that. We'll be there as soon as we're released." He hung up. "They found something."

"What?"

"Don't know, but Heller wants me to see it." Jace paused. "Nurse?"

Seconds later, the nurse reappeared. "Yes, Constable Allen?"

"How soon can we leave?"

"Let me check with the doctor on duty. Miss Kelly is awake and asking for you." She retracted Violet's curtain. "I'll be right back."

Jace swung his legs over the side of the bed, leaning forward. "Vi, how are you feeling?"

"Groggy, but thankful to be alive." Violet

eased herself into a seated position and rubbed her abdomen. "Thank you both for saving my baby. I've never been so scared in my life." Tears flowed down her cheeks.

Jace walked over and sat on her bed, bringing her into his arms. "You're safe now. You'll be staying with us at my place for protection. I can't risk CLS getting to you again."

Violet pulled back. "He targeted me because of my profession and the tox screen, didn't he?"

"That's what we suspect." Jace looked down. "And because of me."

Violet lifted his chin. "Don't blame yourself. This guy is sick." She paused and eyed Scarlet before turning back to Jace. "I need to tell you something when we're alone."

Suddenly, Scarlet had the desire to flee and hide under a rock. Obviously, these two possessed a strong bond. However, Jace's body language and actions revealed only brotherly love.

Had years of experience in Scarlet's profession taught her how to read mannerisms that easily?

One thing was clear—Violet longed for more. The look in the redhead's eyes proved it.

And Scarlet no longer harbored a jealous twinge.

Just sympathy for the woman when she found out Jace only wanted friendship.

Scarlet's phone dinged, announcing a text. She swiped the screen.

Why won't you die? Don't think you can evade me. You won't stand in my way of ridding the island of those wretched women. Jace can't protect you forever. I know where you are and I will kill you.

Scarlet hopped from the hospital bed, head spinning. She clutched the railing to steady herself and held her phone up for Jace to read. "We need to get out of here."

After receiving the doctor's okay to leave the hospital, Jace helped Violet into Taylor's cruiser. Taylor would escort Violet to her home to get some belongings before taking her to Jace's house. Marcy had promised to keep an eye out for them and then lock the premises down. Tight. Jace wasn't taking any risks that CLS would get to his friend again. He'd taken her aside to find out what she wanted to tell him. She'd admitted her crush, but also that she knew he didn't feel the same way. She'd decided in the short time of her abduction that she no longer wanted to be a forensic toxicologist and that her pregnancy had made her think about a career in working with children. Plus, her brother had requested she move to Nova Scotia, so they could be closer together. It had been something she'd been pondering for a few months, and while in the church basement, she'd reached a conclusion. It was time. She was moving. Jace had told her he'd help in any way he could and that he'd miss her, but he totally understood.

It was for the best. His heart belonged to another. But what would happen when Scarlet remembered their rocky relationship in college? His contrary ways had bothered her, and she had let him know. Hopefully, Jace could prove he'd changed since those days.

He stole a peek at Scarlet. She rested her head back. "You sure you're okay to come with me?"

She popped forward. "I'm good. Just waiting for the meds to take this headache away."

"Have any more memories returned?"

She averted her gaze. "Just a few, but nothing about CLS. Did you say there's a counselor I could see?"

"Yes. I'll set something up for you." Jace drove into the abandoned church's parking lot and parked beside Heller's cruiser.

"Appreciate it." Scarlet opened her door. "Let's go see what they found." She stepped outside.

He exited the vehicle. Dusk had come earlier on the cloudy summer day, cooling the temperatures. Jace stared at the unkempt church as a question rose.

How many people had come to Christ in this tiny congregation? What were their stories?

"You coming?" Scarlet's question popped him back to the situation at hand.

His cell phone rang before he could respond. He read the screen. Chief Constable Chris Hopkins from the Saanich detachment. Jace braced himself. Why would he be calling? Jace raised his index finger at Scarlet. "I need to take this call. Just a sec." He punched the answer button. "Good evening, Chief. How can I help you?"

"Allen, I'm so sorry to hear of Ray's death. He was a close friend, and I will miss him." The man's deep voice hitched, and he cleared his throat. "I left a message with Whitney for you to call me."

He kicked himself for not following through. "Sorry, I've been a bit busy."

"I understand. Listen, the reason I'm calling is I'm replacing Ray, but not for a few weeks. I know you were up for a promotion, and he spoke highly of you. He was rough at times, but that was his style."

"He was an outstanding leader, sir."

"Agree. I need someone to lead the team so we can get moving forward on this case. I'm putting you in charge, and if it goes well, you'll be my right-hand man…once we go through the proper procedures, of course."

Jace bristled. How would the others take the chain of command? They already had something against him. "I'd be honored. Thank you."

"I will inform your team of the change. You

will now report to me. Do Ray proud. Please find this killer."

No pressure. "Yes, sir." He clicked off.

Jace stuffed his phone into his pocket and hurried to catch up to Scarlet. "Apparently, I'm now in charge."

"Congratulations."

"Well, not sure how the others will take it."

They climbed the church's steps together. The perilous events from a few hours ago were still fresh in his mind.

Scarlet hesitated. "Are we sure it's okay to enter?"

"Yes, enough time has passed, and the firefighters gave Heller the all clear." He entered the building.

Heller and Lewis hovered around the obliterated door leading to the basement. The explosion had left a gaping hole in the side wall. Heller turned at their approach. "There you are. You guys okay?"

"We're good," Jace said. "What did you find?"

Heller gestured toward the opposite side of the church's sanctuary. "It's through that door."

Jace scratched his head. How had they missed the other door? The discarded boxes reminded him. They'd obviously been stacked in front of the room, blocking their view.

Heller walked through the entrance.

Jace stopped in the doorway and whistled.

Pictures of women coated the walls like wallpaper. Some had their faces crossed off—the victims he'd killed. Jace stepped closer and pulled on gloves. He fingered the peeling paint on the wall. Blank spots were missing between Lila Canfield and Rose Penny's pictures. Pieces of tape still clung, as if he'd yanked them down in a haste before leaving.

Obviously, CLS had put the boxes in front of the door for a reason. He'd wanted to hide the contents, but why abandon them here in this church where police would find them? Unless—

He'd thought the building would be destroyed by the explosion and gas leak, but the police had fouled his plan.

Thankfully.

Different-size seashells, a small battery-operated drill and lengths of crafter's leather rope filled a corner table.

Scarlet drew in a sharp breath beside him. "Wow, this must have been CLS's lair. Why would he choose an abandoned, rickety church?"

"Off the beaten path," Heller said, moving deeper into the narrow room. "Look at this."

Dismantled darts lined another table next to multiple bottles of various drugs and poisons—liquid Xanax, fentanyl, strychnine, cyanide—plus syringes.

"Do you think he made a deadly cocktail out of these? I bet one dose would bring down a seven-hundred-pound grizzly bear." Jace picked up the bottle of powdered strychnine. "I'm pretty sure this was sprinkled on the flowers CLS sent you."

"Probably." Scarlet pointed to the pictures. "Why would he use these to kill a witness but strangle all these women? Why not just poison them? It would be faster."

He shrugged.

She tapped on her cell phone. "I'm going to video call Olive to get her take on what we found."

"Good idea," Jace said.

Seconds later, Scarlet held her phone up. "Olive, Jace and Frank are here. We wanted your impression on what we've found in an abandoned church. I'll walk you through it." Scarlet explained what they suspected and moved around the room, bringing her phone closer to the pictures.

Olive hissed. "Oh, my. This guy is definitely obsessed with the same type of women."

Scarlet scanned the room, including the poison.

"Wait, stop." Olive pointed toward the liquid Xanax. "That one is known on the street as liquid bliss. I'm going to hazard a guess it's what CLS uses to sedate his victims."

"And it doesn't normally show up on tests. Good call." Jace opened a desk drawer and hauled out a folder. "Why do you think he'd take his time with these women before killing them?"

"Pardon the expression, but he enjoys the thrill of the kill. Plus, whoever he's lashing out about from his past obviously made him suffer. He's taking his pain out on these women."

Jace leafed through the folder's contents and held up additional pictures. "Looks like he stalked his victims first. Look at these."

Scarlet brought the phone over so Olive could see what he'd found. Different shots of the women at their places of employment, homes, recreational activities. Everything.

Scarlet pointed to one. "She's new. Do you think this is his next victim?"

Jace nodded. "Probably."

"She fits the MO," Olive said. "Same dark hair and age. I gotta run. My boss is calling me. Talk later."

"You got it, Olly." Scarlet disconnected the video call.

Heller walked over and looked at the woman's picture. "Do you know her, Allen?"

"No, but she looks familiar." Jace shoved more pictures aside and stopped at one of a house on a corner street. The street sign and house number were in clear view. "Wait. I recognize the cable van in front of this house. It's Kinsley Harrison's. I ticketed her for a broken taillight a week ago. It's still not fixed. She acted really suspicious the other day when we were talking to her after the masked assailant ran in her direction."

"You're right," Scarlet said. "She hid something from us. It can't be a coincidence her van is in front of the house CLS appears to be staking out."

"I'm going to look into who owns the property." Jace texted the address to a colleague. "Did you find any other evidence in the church, Heller?"

"Nothing of significance. It appears CLS has been holed up here for quite some time." He pointed to a pile of newspapers. "They date back a year."

Jace's cell phone rang, and he glanced at the caller. Dispatch. Jace put it on speaker. "Allen here."

"You need to get to Aster Beach," Dispatch said. "Coast guard found a body floating in the Pacific Ocean."

The hairs at the back of Jace's neck bristled. *No, Lord. Not another victim.*

THIRTEEN

Jace took the curve to the Aster Beach access road too quickly, the tires screeching. He'd left Heller in charge at the church crime scene. Word had gotten out quickly regarding the leadership change, so Jace braced himself for negative comments. He'd set them aside for now and concentrate on finding CLS.

On their drive over, Lewis had updated them on evidence they'd obtained. Unfortunately, nothing came from the bomb fragments that took the chief's life, and they'd found no fingerprints on the dart rifle—not that Jace expected there would be. He suppressed a groan as frustration mounted. They had to get ahead of CLS. Somehow.

Jace parked in the beach's lot and killed the engine before turning to Scarlet. She reclined against the headrest. "This is our last stop for the day. I promise. I'm sure you're tired."

Scarlet gathered her portfolio. "I'm good. We need to stop this maniac." She exited the cruiser.

He stepped outside into the night. Darkness had fallen like his mood over the urgency of solving this case. *Lord, give me wisdom.* He surveyed the area. A popular French fry restaurant still bustled at the early-evening hour. People came from all over to taste the special sauce this family-owned restaurant boasted about. It had been in their family for over a hundred years. The aroma coming from the establishment enticed his stomach. However, he ignored the hunger pang and gazed at the ocean.

The moon illuminated the water. This was one of his favorite spots, but it was now tainted by death. If they didn't stop the Coastline Strangler soon, all their beaches would be contaminated by recollections of where CLS had dumped his victims.

A search-and-rescue team was gathered at the shore with the coroner, as were constables from the area.

"This way." Jace stepped onto the beach, his boots sinking into the sand. A crowd had gathered around the scene, and one officer tried unsuccessfully to contain the onlookers. Seemed everyone wanted to know what had happened. "Stay close to me and keep your eyes peeled. CLS may be among the crowd. Be careful, though. He's harassing you and won't stop his deadly pursuit. Obviously, he still doesn't realize you have amnesia."

Scarlet hugged her portfolio. "I'll study and draw the crowd. Maybe something will spark a memory."

"Sounds good."

"Jace, buddy." A figure approached. "I hear you're in charge now."

Jace fist-bumped his best friend. "Finn. So good to see you." He turned to Scarlet. "Scarlet, this is rescue specialist Officer Finnegan Jacobs. Finn, this is our forensic artist, Scarlet Wells."

Finn stepped forward. "Pleasure to meet you. I've heard great things about your work."

"Thank you. How do you two know each other?" Scarlet asked.

"Best friends since high school. Played on the football team together." Jace slapped him on the back. "Finn, did you find the victim?"

"Yes. We had reports of a body in the water, so they sent me in. Once we noticed the woman's hair color and the ligature lines on her neck, we guessed she was probably a CLS victim. We were getting ready to transport her when our boat's engine died. We didn't want to waste time waiting on the repairs, so we brought her to shore via a dinghy. We contacted your team and the coroner en route."

"CLS leaves his victims on the beach, though,"

Scarlet said. "What was she doing out in the ocean?"

Finn stared at the water. "It appears he miscalculated the high tides for this shore. She must have washed out to sea when it moved in."

"Did you notice if she had a seashell necklace on?" Jace asked.

"Only a seashell bracelet."

Jace peeked over at Scarlet. "That's odd. He's changed his MO."

"Are you thinking copycat?" Scarlet took out her sketch pad.

"But we've kept that bit of information from the media." Jace scribbled a note. "How would anyone know other than CLS?"

"No idea. I'm going to start diagramming the scene." Scarlet positioned herself with her back to the water, facing the scene, shoreline and bystanders.

Finn turned to Jace. "Bud, I gotta run, but I wanted to tell you something just in case it's approved. I've put in a transfer request to Nova Scotia. It's a promotion if I get it. Plus, you know my family moved back to the east coast a few years ago, so I'll be closer to my sister. She's been struggling since our mother was killed and doesn't have the best relationship with our father."

"From one coast to the other, huh? I don't blame you. Family is the most important thing in our lives." Jace squeezed Finn's shoulder. "I'll be praying you get it but will miss you."

"Ditto. See you at Bible study?"

Jace nodded. "Stay safe."

Finn trotted over to his team.

Jace approached the scene.

Dr. Drew hovered over the woman's body, examining the ligature marks on her neck. Aiden observed the chief coroner's movements carefully.

Scarlet stood off to the side, sketching.

Jace put on gloves and crouched beside the body, studying the woman's face. "What can you tell us about her? Any identification?"

Dr. Drew lifted his gaze, and his glasses slipped to the end of his nose. "Not this time, I'm afraid." He pointed to her neck. "Appears to be the same cause of death."

Scarlet moved closer. "Can you say how long she'd been in the water?"

"Since she has no other visible marks and this is the ocean, I'm guessing not long. The fish would probably have nibbled on her body." Dr. Drew pursed his lips. "However, you know how I hate to guess. I'll learn more once I get her on my table."

"Understood." Jace looked closer at the woman's mouth. "Scarlet, it appears she has the same lipstick on that was at Violet's. Just faded. Plus, the seashell bracelet instead of a necklace tells me CLS is changing things up. Why, is the question."

Scarlet held up her cell phone. "You okay if I take a picture and send to Olive for her opinion?"

"Go ahead. I'd be interested in her thoughts. Hey, did she ever say if Zac got in touch with her?"

"Nothing." Scarlet snapped shots and sent them. "Have the constables found anything else? How can we tell this is the actual beach where CLS left her?"

"We can't. I wonder—"

"Constable Allen, we found something you may want to see." A young female officer approached and gestured for them to follow.

They trudged through the sand to the other side of the beach.

The constable stopped and shone her flashlight on a large piece of driftwood.

A broken seashell necklace dangled from a branch.

An exact match to those found on the other victims.

Scarlet peered out her bedroom patio door, watching the fireflies light up Jace's backyard and illuminate the cliffs in the background. The spectacular display tugged at her heart, creating a desire for peace. Something she'd been missing for the past few days. Did she struggle with stillness and resting in the moment? She had an inkling her personality required something to occupy her every moment of her day. Why she felt this way, she didn't know. The struggle of her lost memories tormented her. She needed to remember. Not so much for herself, but for these women. She owed it to them to recall CLS's face. *Lord, show me what I drew during Lila's interview.* Scarlet thought back to the latest victim and tried to imagine the horror she must have gone through. It was clear they'd found the correct beach after examining the seashell necklace. It had obviously gotten snagged on the driftwood as her body was swept out to sea.

Jace had bagged it into evidence, but they doubted they'd get any prints off it. The combination of it being in the water and the small size of the seashells eliminated the possibility. Plus, CLS was too clever to construct necklaces without wearing gloves.

Their hopes remained locked in Scarlet's faulty mind.

No pressure.

Jace had booked an appointment for Scarlet to talk to their counselor tomorrow. After they left the scene and ate an order of fries, Jace brought her back to his fortress. He'd assured her his constables would patrol his street frequently and his surveillance equipment was top-notch. They were safe.

Scarlet lounged in the plush chair next to the window in the comfortable spare bedroom and opened her sketch pad. She put in her earbuds, turned her music on and flipped through each drawing, studying faces and scenes, hoping for a trigger. A clue. Anything to help in the case.

Wait—she stopped at the third sketch and peered at the crowd, then flipped back through the other two.

She'd drawn the same hooded person in some of the pictures. The man had his hands shoved into his jeans pockets, observing the scene.

The Coastline Strangler had been there multiple times. Right under their noses.

Scarlet peered closer at him. His hoodie was too far down and she hadn't been able to draw much of his face, but his small stature fit Olive's profile. She slammed her sketchbook closed and read the time on her watch. Too late now to show Jace. She'd do it in the morning.

Not that it helped identify CLS, but next time perhaps Jace could get his constables to keep a close eye out for someone with this description. CLS would want to keep his identity concealed, so he'd definitely need to wear a hoodie, and in the summer heat, that would stand out.

Scarlet's cell phone played its jangling ring, announcing an incoming video call. She turned her music off and swiped at the screen. Olive. Scarlet cleared her throat and hit the button. "Hey, Olly. You're up late. Isn't it like one in the morning there?"

Olive was propped up against a headboard, her pink owl pajamas showing on the screen. "Couldn't sleep and you were on my mind, so I had to make sure you were okay. Did you and Jace find anything else at the scene?"

"Yes, the necklace, which must have snagged on a piece of driftwood when the woman's body swept into the water. We're confused why CLS has changed his MO by adding lipstick and a matching piece of jewelry. Did you see the picture I sent? What do you think, in your professional opinion?"

"He's getting overconfident and is enjoying the attention. I've been following his social media accounts, and he's boasting about how he's evading capture."

"What? Please tell me you didn't friend him." Scarlet flipped open her sketchbook.

"Nope, just lurking." She made a funny face. "Don't worry, Zac has been hovering. I can't believe Jace sent my ex, of all people, to guard me."

"Don't forget Ziva. Wait, aren't you scared of dogs?"

Olive sat upright. "You remembered that?"

"I did, but I don't know how. Just wish my mind would speed up the process. I need to remember CLS's face." She held up one of her drawings. "Speaking of him, I discovered tonight there's one person who's been in the crowd of bystanders in three of my sketches." She pointed. "There."

"Wow, his presence solidifies my assessment of him injecting himself into the investigation." She slumped back again. "You need to catch him, sis. Did you identify his latest victim?"

"Not yet. Jace is also running down a lead from the pictures we found at the church. Hopefully, we'll know more tomorrow."

Olive pressed her face closer to the screen.

Scarlet laughed. "What are you doing?"

"Trying to see what your room looks like."

"It's gorgeous and gigantic. You should see Jace's house. Amazing. Here, let me show you some." Scarlet stood and swiveled the camera's direction, walking through the room slowly.

She opened the patio door and stepped out onto the balcony. "Can't stay out here long or Jace will have my hide. I wanted to show you the cliffs." She did a panorama shot.

Olive whistled. "Gorgeous. Hey, are those fireflies?"

"They are. Remember how we used to try and catch them?" Scarlet swiveled the lens around and grinned. "I just remembered something else."

Olive pumped her fist in the air. "Yay, now get back inside."

Scarlet obeyed, hope surging through her. "Can you tell me more about Mom and Dad? I remembered Mom was diagnosed with Alzheimer's."

Olive spent the next few minutes telling her

more about their parents and how their mother's memories had slowly started failing at age sixty-three. "She's now in a nursing home and barely recognizes Dad or me."

Scarlet sank into the chair, her chest closing in on her suddenly. *Why can't I remember that? Mom, is this what you go through every day?*

Tears welled at the thought of her mother forgetting her loved ones. This experience gave Scarlet a taste of how the woman must have felt to lose her identity. However, for Evelyn Wells, it would have been magnified, as with Alzheimer's the forgetfulness tormented the mind slowly. Remembering and then not remembering must have been agony.

Scarlet clutched the armrest as a wave of sadness gripped her heart, blurring her vision. A question rose—why did God allow such heartbreaking illnesses?

Olive yawned, invading Scarlet's thoughts. "I'm sorry, sis. Time for bed. Night. Love you."

"Love you more." The expression rolled off Scarlet's tongue so easily, it had to be one of their sayings to each other. Sisters' bond and all.

Olive giggled and waved goodbye before her beautiful face disappeared from the screen.

Time for bed. Scarlet rose from her chair.

The video chat jangled again. Scarlet hit the button without looking at the screen. "What did you forget, sis?"

"Not your sis," the distorted voice said.

Scarlet sucked in a breath and glanced at the screen.

A masked head appeared, eyes peeking through the slits.

Her legs weakened. "How did you get this number?"

"I have my ways. After all, I'm the Coastline Strangler."

Scarlet stumbled toward the door. She had to get to Jace. Now.

"Stay where you are, missy, or Charlie will pay the price."

Scarlet skidded to a stop. How did the man discover her location? She wouldn't put the boy at risk. An idea formed. Maybe she could use this call to their advantage. Figure out more clues from the notorious killer. "Tell me. Why do you choose dark-haired women in their late twenties?"

He harrumphed. "They are evil. That's why."

"Why are they evil?"

"Are you psychoanalyzing me, like your sister? By the way, she's very pretty."

She hissed a breath through her teeth. "Leave. My. Sister. Alone."

"She's safe. For now." He wheezed as the screen on his phone bounced.

He was running.

She peered closer, trying to determine his location. "You haven't answered my question. Do these women remind you of your mother?"

He stopped.

Bingo.

"So, it *is* your mother. What did she do to you? I know it had something to do with a beach, or why else do you leave the women there with a seashell necklace?"

"You're smart. I like you, Scarlet Wells. Too bad you have to die."

Scarlet's legs wobbled, and she held on to the bed's wooden foot post. "You're evading the question again. Why these women?"

The eyes behind the slits narrowed. "They were vixens. That's why. My mission is to remove them all from Vancouver Island."

Had these women flirted with him? Was that why he chose them? Another question rose. "Is your mother a flirt, too?"

"You'll get nothing more from me tonight, Miss Scarlet." He snickered. "I just wanted to say hi. You can't stay locked up in that palace for long."

She cringed at his tone. "What do you want from me?"

"That's easy. For you to die. However, it's not quite your moment yet." He started running again. "I left you a present for your appointed time on the patio. Good night." He ended the call.

Scarlet's breath hitched. Dare she look? Was he still out there?

She snapped on the outside light and peered onto the deck.

A seashell necklace hung from the railing at the corner of the balcony.

Scarlet dropped to her knees.

The Coastline Strangler had crafted a necklace for her burial.

FOURTEEN

Frantic, persistent pounding woke Jace from a dead sleep.

"Jace, wake up," Scarlet yelled.

He jerked upright and staggered to the door, yanking it open.

Scarlet stood in his entryway with a seashell necklace dangling from one hand, her gun in the other. She held up the piece of jewelry. "CLS was out there. He video called me and left me this on the patio railing."

"*What?*" Jace hustled to his closet and took his Glock 17 out from his locked safe hidden behind his wardrobe, keeping it by his side.

Scarlet stepped back into the hallway. "I'm pretty sure he's gone."

Jace kept his fisted hands by his sides. "Why didn't you come get me?"

"He threatened Charlie's life. I didn't want to take the risk."

Jace nudged her forward. "I need to check the

cameras to ensure he's gone and call my team. First, I want to make sure Charlie, Marcy and Vi are safe."

She nodded.

After ensuring they all slept soundly, Jace and Scarlet cleared the house. The constable in the cruiser outside his house checked the perimeter, but they reported nothing suspicious. The alarm was still set, so how had CLS gotten past the outside motion sensors to leave the necklace on Scarlet's patio? Perhaps the video would tell them more and shed some light on how CLS had infiltrated his life. On the way to the equipment room, Jace called the constable on duty to relay the information and requested they make more frequent patrol stops around the area.

Jace opened the door and flicked on the light. "Let's check the cameras, but tell me everything about your conversation with CLS." He pulled out a gamer chair and gestured for her to sit.

Scarlet plunked herself down. "Olive and I video chatted and hung up. The phone rang seconds later, and I thought it was her calling back, so I didn't even look at the screen. He was masked and used some kind of voice-changer app."

"Did you see his eyes?"

"Barely. The slits in the mask were small. After he warned me he'd go after Charlie if I left the room, I used the call to find out information."

Smart thinking. He wiggled the mouse to bring his system to life. "Good girl. What did you find out?"

Scarlet told him about CLS's mother and how he felt it was his mission to eliminate the island of all vixen women. She also relayed information she'd received from her sister on CLS's bold changes to his MO and about her sketches of the hooded bystander at some of the crime scenes.

Jace leaned back and exhaled loudly. "Wow. Productive evening. That's amazing you got that out of him." He squeezed her shoulder. "I believe we're getting closer to catching him, but are you okay? This must have shaken you."

"It did at first, but I'm more determined to catch this lunatic. He truly is deranged in his attitude toward women." She paused. "I need to get a phone CLS doesn't know about."

"I can help with that." Jace opened a drawer full of cell phones.

Scarlet tilted her head as her lips turned upward, exploding into an enchanting grin.

He ignored what it did to his insides and dug one out. "Yes, I'm obsessed. I have several private phones stashed throughout the house. You can never be too safe." He failed to include details about his anxiety due to his childhood abduction. Even at a young age, he'd seen how it had affected his parents, instilling fear into him.

It festered and grew into his adulthood, prompting his overcautious state of mind.

Jace keyed on one of the phones and handed it to her. "Here. I added in my personal unlisted number, too. I keep it in the kitchen in case Marcy requires an extra one."

She smirked. "Wow. You *are* obsessed."

Jace chuckled and brought all the cameras into view. "Okay, what time did CLS call?"

"Ten thirty."

"Let's see if we can find him." He rewound the footage from the front entrance and hit Play. Nothing out of the ordinary appeared. Had CLS come up the cliffs from the beach? Jace switched cameras and peered out. Darkness followed by flashes from fireflies. He hit Rewind and then Play.

Scarlet leaned closer. "Wait. Stop. Look at the corner of the screen."

Jace hit Stop and zoomed in. A darkened figure appeared over the cliff's walkway and came up to the gate to Jace's backyard. The assailant was dressed in black, head to toe. He removed a device and typed on a keypad. Seconds later, he looked directly into the camera, the whites of his eyes shining. Jace could almost see the sneer behind his mask. Seconds later, the footage darkened.

Jace switched to another camera. It, too, went

black. "Wait, how did CLS know exactly where my cameras are?"

Movement sounded behind them, and Jace picked up his weapon, spinning around in his chair. He raised his gun.

Marcy held up her hands. "It's just me."

Jace set his gun on the desk. "Don't sneak up like that. Why are you out of bed?"

"I thought I heard something and came to investigate." Marcy peered at the screen. "What's going on?"

Jace raked his fingers through his hair. "CLS somehow bypassed my motion sensors and left Scarlet a present on her balcony."

Marcy grabbed Scarlet's arm. "Dear, are you okay?"

"Just a bit shaken. We're trying to figure out how he discovered the camera locations." Scarlet slouched in the chair.

Marcy inhaled a quick breath. "I think I know."

"How?" Jace asked.

"I'm so sorry. This totally slipped my mind. The other day I heard a buzzing noise. Charlie and I walked outside to see what it was. Someone was flying a drone over the property."

Jace popped out of his seat. "Why didn't you tell me sooner?" His harsh tone conveyed his sudden panicked state.

Scarlet's eyes widened at his sharp reaction. *Not good, Jace. Rein it in.* He hugged Marcy.

"I'm sorry. I didn't mean to sound so angry. I'm just concerned for your safety."

"It's okay. I understand, Jace. There's a lot at stake."

"Tell me what happened."

"It was about nine thirty in the morning. Charlie saw it first and told me what it was. How does a five-year-old know what a drone is?"

"Too much TV, I guess." Jace turned to Scarlet. "So, CLS used a drone, obviously equipped with a camera, to recon the place. It's probably also how he got the shot of Charlie on the beach. Clever." He picked up his cell phone. "I need to get more patrols out here. Show me where CLS left the necklace."

After reassuring Marcy the suspect was gone and telling her to go back to bed, Jace followed Scarlet through her guest bedroom and onto the patio.

Scarlet pointed to the decorative wrought iron tip on the patio railing. "It was hanging there."

Jace knelt to check the angle. "How did you not hear him?"

"I was listening to music earlier, but my question is, how did he get up here? There are no stairs."

Jace moved to the edge and leaned over. "My guess is the wrought iron trellis. My parents put in a sturdy one for Mom's flower vines, as she didn't want to have to replace it. Heath and I used to climb down them at night to sneak out."

She clasped her hand over her mouth. Obviously to suppress her laughter.

"Don't laugh. We never got caught. Let's get back to safety, shall we?"

Scarlet took a step but bumped into the small patio table and stumbled into his arms.

He tightened his hold on her, tucking a black strand of hair behind her ear.

A soft cry escaped her lips. "I'm sorry about that."

He smiled. Her smoky voice sent a shiver down his spine. He'd forgotten how he loved the raspiness in her tone. That, along with her button-brown eyes and raven hair, had sent his heart fluttering all those years ago when they first met in college. Things went downhill after that. His attitude had irritated her, and he didn't blame her. He hated the man—boy—he was back then. What would happen once Scarlet remembered his wayward days? They had butted heads on everything from sports to college classes to movies. However, in her defense, he had always had to be right. Another trait he had hated about himself. After learning some lessons in life, he'd changed his ways.

"Nothing to be sorry about." He eyed her lips and imagined what it would be like to kiss her. An image of Rene flashed through his mind, and he stepped away. He couldn't take another rejection.

Something flashed in her eyes. Disappointment?

Her expression tugged at his heart, almost making him pull her back into his arms, but he held strong.

After all, his heart wasn't all that was at stake.

He wouldn't put Charlie through anything else.

Scarlet woke to a pitter-patter of feet outside her bedroom, followed by continuous banging on the door. She sat upright. Had she overslept? She checked the time on her cell phone. Six forty-five a.m. She thought back to last night's intimate moment. She was positive Jace had been about to kiss her, but then he'd backed away. The question was…had she wanted him to?

"Miss Scarlet, time for brekky." Charlie pounded again.

Both this boy and his father knew how to capture her heart in a short time frame. *Scarlet, you'll be returning to Whitehorse soon. You can't get close.*

She threw the covers off and stepped out of bed. "Coming, Charlie."

After hustling to get dressed, Scarlet shuffled into the kitchen and was greeted by a disheveled, curly-haired five-year-old. He hugged her legs, melting her resolve to stay strong.

"Morning, bud." Scarlet tousled his curls.

"I made you breakfast, Miss Scarlet." He took her hand and tugged her forward. "Let's sit."

"What did you make me, Charlie?" She eyed Jace.

He winked.

Her pulse quickened. She willed it to slow down. *He's not interested.*

Charlie climbed into his chair. "Cereal."

Scarlet chuckled.

Jace's cell phone chimed, and he read the screen. He bounded upright. "Sorry, bud. We gotta get to work." He turned to Scarlet. "We got an identification on the woman from last night."

Scarlet noticed he chose his words carefully in front of his son. "I'll get my things and meet you in the car."

Ten minutes later, Scarlet followed Jace into the police station and their task force command center, hot beverages in hand. The team had been assembled to go over the latest development.

Jace set up his laptop and gestured everyone to sit. "We've had some interesting situations arise. First, CLS's latest victim was Beth Harrison, Kinsley Harrison's sister. The home in the picture we found at the church was Beth's. That's why the cable van was there. This proves CLS is stalking his victims before abducting them."

"Has anyone spoken to Kinsley?" Scarlet asked. "She was pretty evasive the other day."

Gail raised her hand. "I did. She's a friend of mine. Kinsley confessed she'd been hooking up free cable at her sister's house and noticed someone staking out the place, but she didn't want to say anything because her boss would have fired her. She couldn't identify the man in the car, and when she approached him, he sped off. She's devastated at the loss of her sister and not involved in any other way."

"Scarlet, tell the group what you found out from CLS last night." Jace sipped his tea.

Gail's gaze snapped to Scarlet's. "You were talking to him?"

Scarlet opened her sketch pad. "Yes, he video called me. Wore a mask and used a voice-changer app. He confessed he targets vixen-type women and wants to rid the island of them. Also, I've confirmed the female figure who is his inspiration is his mother. Not sure what she did to him. Can you find out if Beth recently visited a bar? Or somewhere else? Maybe she flirted with him. CLS picked her for a reason." She held her drawings up, flipping the pages. "I've been sketching and diagramming the crime scenes and noticed the same hooded figure has been present at some of them. CLS is definitely watching us."

Gail keyed on her phone. "I'll see if Kinsley

knows Beth's recent whereabouts. Perhaps we can narrow down where CLS is meeting his victims."

"Although, since he's killing across the island, that might be hard," Jace said. "However, if we can determine if it's a bar or somewhere else, we can keep close tabs on them. Share that with the media and ask women to be careful."

Doug added a "possible locations" column to their whiteboard. "Agreed."

Jace held an evidence bag in the air. "He left this for Scarlet and told her he'd be coming after her. We need to ensure she's protected at all times."

Frank leaned forward. "Have any memories returned?"

Scarlet chewed the inside of her cheek. Would they judge her for not remembering? "Not about him. I have an appointment this afternoon that will hopefully help." *Lord, make it happen. We need a win here.*

Jace handed the necklace evidence bag to Frank. "Can you take this to Forensics?"

The man's eyes narrowed. "Yes, sir."

Ouch. Seemed the constable didn't like the switch in command. Scarlet eyed Jace's face. His contorted expression revealed his hurt, but he quickly replaced it with determination.

"Okay, I need to clear the air. I know this change of leadership has been hard on the team.

I'm sorry it had to happen this way, but we need to work together. The community is depending on us." Jace stared at each constable separately before continuing. "Can we do that?"

Good for him. Scarlet admired his obvious willingness to set his personal feelings aside for the sake of the case.

The team nodded.

"Okay, let's get to work, shall we?" Jace closed his laptop.

The constables sprinted from the room, almost bumping into Whitney as she rushed through the door. "Boss man, there's a woman on the tip line I think you need to talk to. Line four."

Jace brought the conference phone closer to him. "Thanks, Whitney. We've got it."

She nodded and left the room.

Jace hit the button. "Constable Allen here. How may I help you?"

The woman cleared her throat. "My name is Amy Brampton, and I believe the Coastline Strangler may be my dead son."

Jace straightened. This might be the break they needed.

"What makes you think that, Miss Brampton?" Jace asked.

"It's Mrs. Brampton. I got married three weeks ago."

Scarlet reviewed the timeline on their board. The killings had restarted two weeks ago.

Could this have been CLS's trigger and behind the acceleration of kills?

"Sorry. Mrs. Brampton." Jace jotted in his notebook. "Tell me why you think our killer is your son, and what's his name?"

"Kevin Vale. Because the news just reported that CLS places seashell necklaces on his victims."

Jace's gaze snapped to hers. The obvious same question resonated on his crinkled forehead.

How was that information leaked? The team had kept it from the media.

Scarlet wrote "Kevin Vale" in her notebook.

Jace tapped his pencil. "But that still proves nothing. There are many seashell necklaces out there."

"My son collected seashells and made me the same ones when he was little," Amy said. "He used a specific knot. Just like the one they showed on the news."

Jace snapped his pencil in two, showing his frustration at this leak.

Scarlet scribbled "she said dead son" on a piece of paper and raised it.

Jace nodded. "Mrs. Brampton, you mentioned your son was deceased. What makes you think he's alive and the killer?"

"I was a single mother and struggled financially. Kevin and I fought a lot, and he ran away in his early teens. I tried to find him but couldn't.

Seemed he didn't want me to." Her voice quivered. "Years later, I received a visit from an army officer. Apparently, Kevin had enlisted and was killed in a roadside bombing overseas. They brought me his dog tags."

"I'm sorry for your loss. Do you have any pictures of Kevin?" Jace asked.

"Only as a five-year-old. Our apartment building burned down, and I could only save the one."

Scarlet put the phone on mute. "Let me come with you when you talk with her. I'm good at reading body language and can tell when someone is lying. A forensic artist's skill."

Jace nodded and unmuted. "We're coming to you. Can you tell me where you live? Also, please text me the picture." He spieled off his cell number.

She agreed and gave them her address.

Twenty minutes later, Jace parked along the roadside in front of Amy Brampton's luxurious home. A question rose in Scarlet's mind.

Had she married into money? Was that what triggered CLS? Jealousy over his mother's new wealth?

Jace had done a search on Kevin Vale and shared the army article he'd found. Most of the team had died in the bombing. All but two officers. The unit appeared in a picture in full gear, complete with masks and goggles. Their faces were hidden. He'd also texted her Kevin's picture. They'd studied the photo together. Mother and son on a beach, appearing to look happy. However, the son's forced smile told Scarlet's intuition otherwise. Had this been the start of his internal hatred of women? What had the mother done to deserve her son's wrath?

Jace shut the engine off. "This new information could break this case wide-open. But I need to find out how the media got wind of the seashells."

Scarlet held up her phone. "I just did. CLS is bragging about how close he got to a constable. He posted a picture of the necklace hanging on my patio."

He twisted his hands on the wheel. "I need to end CLS's madness."

Scarlet squeezed his muscular bicep. "You will. You're good at what you do. Even though I don't remember you from college, I'm proud of who you've become. A great constable full of compassion."

He averted his eyes.

But not before she noticed his twisted expression. What emotion had just passed over his face? Regret?

Jace opened his door. "Thanks. Let's go talk to CLS's mother."

They exited the vehicle. Scarlet stepped onto the grass.

A humming noise sounded nearby.

What was—

Scarlet looked upward.

A low-flying drone approached the property, zooming toward Amy's home at full speed. The intent was clear.

Jace yanked her backward. "Get down!"

Together, they dropped to the pavement as the house exploded.

FIFTEEN

Jace's eardrums pounded from their dive to the ground and the enormous, roaring explosion. He rolled onto his back and stared into the now hazy sky, trying to calm his rapid pulse. He breathed in. Out. After a few seconds, he ignored the migraine creeping in and sat upright. He turned to Scarlet. "You hurt?"

She eased herself into a standing position and wiped dust from her dark pants. "Fine. Tired of dodging bullets, gas leaks and now a bomb-carrying drone."

"Agree. It's been a strange few days, that's for sure." He withdrew his cell phone. "I'll call it in." He reported the explosion, requesting backup and emergency services, then turned to Scarlet. "I'm going to approach the house. You stay here."

"No. It's not safe." She pointed. "Look at it. The house is gone."

"I need to see if there's any possibility someone survived."

"Then, I'm coming with you and don't stop me." Scarlet proceeded toward the home.

The stubborn demeanor he remembered from their college days had resurfaced. He shook his head and followed her up the laneway toward the house. He hustled to get in front of her, his desire to protect her returning.

He stopped short. A gigantic hole stood where the home had been.

No way anyone had survived this obliteration.

The drone had taken out its target.

Jace cemented his closed fists at his side as tightness clawed his chest. Had CLS done the unspeakable and killed his own mother? Why now? Was there something in her house that would have identified him? And more importantly—

How had he known she'd called them?

These questions plagued his mind, but for now, he wanted to get Scarlet back to safety. CLS might still be in the area. The killer had proved he was always watching.

Somehow.

Jace turned. "No way Amy survived. We need to wait for the firefighters."

Scarlet dropped to her knees and held her head in her hands.

He crouched beside her. "What's wrong?"

She lifted her face, tears cascading down her cheeks. "How many more lives will he take?"

He brought her to her feet and wrapped his arms around her. "We'll catch him. He will make a mistake." Determination stiffened his muscles.

Sirens blared in the background.

He stepped away from their embrace. "Let's move to the street and let the firefighters do their jobs. My team is also on the way."

She nodded and wiped her tears. "I'm sorry for getting emotional. With my amnesia and now this, it just overwhelmed me."

He caressed her cheek. "You're human. It's understandable."

The fire trucks sped down the street and stopped next to the hydrant. Firefighters hopped down from their vehicle, racing to get their hose set up to extinguish the smoldering flames.

The fire chief approached the duo. "You both okay? What happened?"

"Drone loaded with a bomb took out the house," Jace said. "Thankfully, we were still on the street when it happened."

"Drone? Well, that's not something you see every day." The chief gazed at the desecrated home. "This will most likely be a search-and-recovery situation. Probably no survivors."

Jace's team arrived.

"Agreed." Jace handed his business card to the chief. "Let me know if you find anything you feel could be relevant to the Coastline Strangler case.

Specifically, any bodies found in the wreckage. We believe this was his mother's house."

The man's jaw dropped. "That information wasn't given. I will keep your team updated on what we discover." He walked to his men.

Jace gestured toward the constables. "Let's see if any of them have new information."

Jace and Scarlet walked to where his team stood, observing the scene.

Heller whistled. "Wow. I can't believe this happened. How did we find out about his mother?"

Jace explained the conversation they'd had with Amy. "What we don't know is how CLS knew we were coming here. We have to find out how information is leaking from our station."

Lewis stood with his hand on his hips. "It isn't coming from us, Allen. We would never divulge information about a case."

"Not intentionally." Taylor gestured toward Scarlet. "What about her? After all, we really don't know her well."

Scarlet's faced reddened, and she stepped forward.

Jace held her back. "It. Is. Not. Scarlet."

Taylor's gaze held his. "Are you sure?"

He waggled his finger at Taylor. "I've known her since our college years and can vouch for her."

"Okay, I'm right here and can defend myself."

Scarlet turned to Taylor. "I assure you, the leak is not me. I want to stop CLS from killing just as much as you do."

"Now that we got that out of the way, Taylor, can you examine all the lines going in and out of the station for wiretaps? Also, check Amy Brampton's line." Jace eyed the property. "If you can."

"On it." She took a step but turned. "Oh, I found out from Kinsley her sister had been visiting King Gentian's Bar frequently. Maybe send someone to stake it out." She ran to her cruiser and sped off.

Jace turned to Heller and Lewis. "Can you arrange for officers around the island to check on bars? That could be where CLS is picking his victims. Interview the bartenders and get back to me."

The duo left together.

"What's up for us?" Scarlet asked.

"I'm going to investigate Kevin Vale's supposed death a little closer. Something doesn't sit right with me." Jace read his watch. "You have an appointment soon."

"Wait, I just had an idea." She held out the picture Amy sent. "I can use this to create an age progression sketch. That might help us identify CLS."

"Awesome." He leaned closer. "Wait, zoom in on Amy's face."

She complied and held it up again. "Why?"

He pointed to the woman in the photo. "Check out her lipstick color. It looks like rouge sang d'assassin."

Her eyes widened. "This confirms Amy Brampton was CLS's mother. Let's go. I want to get started on my sketch before my meeting."

Jace and Scarlet hurried to his cruiser, a thought tumbling through his mind.

Maybe they were close to catching the Coastline Strangler.

Scarlet eased down on the counselor's plush high-back chair midafternoon and studied the woman's plaques. Certificates denoting Dr. Power's degrees and accomplishments lined the walls, relaxing Scarlet's mind. Her hesitation was not of talking to the doctor, but of what she would remember. Would any flashbacks scare her or help her? Then again, that was why she required this session. For the sake of the island's women, Scarlet had to identify CLS.

"Miss Wells, I understand you recently suffered an injury that left you with amnesia. How are you feeling?" Dr. Power positioned herself in the opposite chair and crossed her legs, tablet in hand.

"Please, call me Scarlet." She white-knuckled

the armrests. "Frustrated. Useless. Scared. All rolled up into one."

"Tell me more." She leaned forward. "Anything you say here will be kept in confidence."

"Good. I can't really discuss the case's details, but I interviewed a witness who survived a horrific event and asked her to describe her attacker. I drew his face, but he somehow found out her location, killed her and tried to kill me. He then burned the composite sketch, and I lost my memory of his face." Scarlet rubbed her temples. "Now I can't help identify him, and women are still dying. It's all my fault."

"Scarlet, your attacker's to blame." The doctor sat back and keyed a note into her tablet. "That's what I'm here to do—help you regain what he stole. Do you remember anything from your childhood?"

"Bits and pieces have slowly returned within the past day or so. How can you help?"

"I'm going to get you to relax and take you back to the moment you lost your memory. Do you remember anything at all from that time?"

"Just when I first started to draw." Scarlet exhaled slowly. "Will the memories come back immediately?"

"Not necessarily, or if at all. It's different for everyone. You ready?"

Scarlet nodded.

"Okay, I want you to rest your head against the seat and close your eyes." Dr. Power steadied her fingers on the keyboard.

Scarlet reclined and shut her eyes.

"Good. Take a few inhales and exhales."

Scarlet obeyed.

"Listen only to the sound of my voice." She paused. "I want you to go back to the time when you began sketching the suspect. I realize you don't remember, but picture the scene in the way you *think* it happened. Forensic artists are good at getting every detail."

Scarlet thought of the moment she'd remembered recently. She visualized herself sitting in a chair, drawing, sketch pad and pencil in hand. That was all. "Okay, I'm there."

"Good. Take a moment and just concentrate. Let it happen naturally." Dr. Power's voice softened.

Scarlet continued to inhale and exhale slowly to calm her rapid pulse. She walked through the process she used to question a witness and then drawing one feature at a time. Minutes passed.

Nothing else came. Scarlet fidgeted in her chair.

"Stay calm. I can tell you're getting restless again. Concentrate. Breathe."

Eyes formed in her mind, appearing on her sketch pad. Evil, creepy eyes. CLS's eyes. A tingle crept through her spine as an overwhelming, frantic apprehension consumed her body.

Scarlet jerked upright. "I see his eyes!"

"That's good. Anything else?"

Scarlet dug deep into the recesses of her brain but failed to come up with more. She shook her head. "I need to go draw the eyes before I forget them again."

Dr. Power stood. "You made good progress, and more might come later. Just remember to let your memories come naturally."

Fifteen minutes after her session, Scarlet sat at a table in the corner of an office at the Coral Bay PD with her back to Jacc as he spoke in low tones on his phone. She required a distraction-free environment in her task of drawing CLS's eyes, so they'd secluded themselves in the room. She wanted to get it right. Scarlet prayed this first step in remembering wouldn't be the last. Dr. Power had given her memory exercises to try to improve her recollections.

She picked up her pencil and sketched, creating the same eerie eyes she'd seen minutes ago. She prayed the rest of CLS's face would follow soon. Her heart palpitated, the sudden wave of panic from earlier returning tenfold. Had this been the emotion she experienced when interviewing Lila? She gripped the edges of the desk and breathed in to steady her pulse.

"You okay?" Jace said, squeezing her shoulder.

She startled and rolled back. "Don't sneak up on me like that." She immediately regretted her harsh tone. "I'm sorry. I'm remembering the panic I felt after seeing these eyes." She passed him her sketch.

Jace sat in his desk chair. "I can see why. Creepy. Did you remember more?"

"Not yet, but Dr. Power said it may happen. Please pray it does."

He handed the sketch pad back to her. "Do you believe in prayer?"

She hesitated, as she still failed to remember if she had faith. "Honestly, I'm not sure. I feel like I do, but how can I trust my fractured memories?"

"You can trust God." He paused. "Well, I confess I've struggled lately. So much has happened in this case that I wonder why God allows such evil in our world. I feel like a terrible Christian, but I'm pretty sure I'm not the only one who does." He smiled. "There's a Bible in your room at my place if you want to read it. I'm praying."

"Thank you." She took out her tablet from her bag. "I'm going to work on the age progression sketch from Kevin's picture."

"Sounds good. I'm tracking down someone in the army and hoping there's a coroner's report included in their documentation. I'll keep you updated." He returned to work.

Scarlet sent Kevin's photo to her tablet and enhanced the image, studying his face. She also researched the age progression process to refresh her faulty mind. She knew forensic artists were trained to understand how the face ages, but she wanted to do the sketch correctly—the first time. Many were counting on her, including Jace.

And for some reason…she did not want to disappoint him.

Or herself.

She moved the enlarged picture to reveal Amy Brampton's younger face and tensed.

How had Scarlet missed the smirk on the woman's bright red lips or the fact that the mother's gaze was focused on something in the distance? It raised a question.

Who had taken the picture?

She picked up her tablet and walked to Jace's desk, holding it up. "Check this out. Amy isn't even looking at the camera or her son. It's like she's not focused on him but something or someone else."

Jace peered closer. "Good call. We need—"

Shots boomed in the hallway. Their office door slammed shut, followed by something being hauled in front of the entrance.

Jace bolted out of his chair and reached for the door handle. "It's stuck."

Someone had blocked their exit.

A whoosh sounded.

Jace turned the knob, only to release it again. "Fire!"

Smoke slithered under the door like a venomous snake.

Images of the bonfire that had killed Becky flashed in Scarlet's mind, and she sank to the floor, holding her head. From what Olive had told her, Scarlet's worst fear now consumed the station.

And they were locked in.

SIXTEEN

Nausea bull-rushed Scarlet, and she swallowed hard, pushing it down. Her bonfire tragedy resurfaced in an instant, along with her entire childhood. Flashes of Becky's scorched body floated in her vision, along with the horror from the night that had created her fear of fire. Her friends had only wanted to enjoy s'mores, but when they'd been impatient for more flames, Scarlet had brought a jerrican full of diesel fuel too close. She'd left them for only a few minutes. The explosion had propelled Scarlet backward but had engulfed her best friend, snuffing the life out of her. Becky's screams tore through Scarlet's mind and she covered her ears, as if she could still hear the young girl's helpless cries, reliving the moment. The firefighters had arrived too late to save her friend.

Jace knelt beside her, rubbing her back. "It's going to be okay."

"I. Remember," Scarlet sobbed. "I remember

the explosion that killed my friend. Need. To. Escape. Now." Her garbled words revealed her panicked state.

Smoke continued to rise through the door.

Fires had a consuming effect on her, and her need for escape escalated.

"Check Ray's locker in the corner for clothes and stuff them under the door. I'm calling Lewis." He punched in a number. "Come on, pick up."

Had CLS gotten to the others in the building?

"I'm trying Taylor," he said. "Gail! Where are you?" He hit Speaker. "We're trapped in Ray's office, and smoke is coming in fast."

"I just arrived through the back door." Gail sounded out of breath. "What's going on?"

"I heard gunshots and then the office door slammed shut, blocking our escape."

"No!" Gail screamed. "Whitney's been hit. Lewis isn't at his desk."

"Be careful. The suspect may still be in the building."

Scarlet opened the steel locker. A jacket and uniform shirt hung on a hook. She reached up and tugged them down before making her way over to the door. She stuffed the jacket in the crack, blocking the fumes.

She hoped.

Shots boomed through the phone's speaker.

"Gail," Jace yelled.

Panting sounded, as if she was running. "I'm

here. The hooded suspect just shot at me and ran out the door. I'm in pursuit. Firefighters are on their way to you. Hold tight." She punched off.

The fumes continued to seep inside from under the door. The fabric wasn't enough to block its entrance.

Scarlet coughed and placed the uniform shirt over her mouth. Spots danced in her vision through the smoky room, and her head spun, fumes overpowering her consciousness. She yanked Jace's hand. "Can't breathe."

He wrapped his arm around her, bringing her close. "Don't give up. Help is on the way."

She peered up at him. Would his handsome face be the last thing she'd see before succumbing to the smoke? How had her feelings for this man grown so quickly over the past few days? Was it their underlying chemistry from their college days that sparked their current flame?

Jace caressed her face as their gazes locked and his eyes moved to her lips.

Was he going to kiss her in a room filled with smoke at a time like this?

An image formed in her mind of them fighting over a college assignment while studying in a library. She'd caught him eyeing her mouth the same way he was now and had guessed he had a crush on her. She recalled the way he'd dated woman after woman—it had disgusted her, but she couldn't help her attraction. Then and now.

Her response had been to throw her textbook at him, hitting him square in the head. Right away, she'd been mortified at her actions and fled the room. Memories returned, of their constant bickering, and remorse pulled her back from his embrace.

Remorse not over his actions, but hers. She now remembered him for the arrogant boy he'd been, but she knew that part of him had been replaced by a compassionate man and father. Someone she could see spending her life with—forever.

However, Brandon, and the secret she now recalled, had robbed her of her ability to ever trust another man. That, compounded with her disgust at herself, closed off her heart to any possibilities with Jace Allen.

Pounding on the door stifled any further recollections.

That and the disappointed, stony expression shadowing his face.

Once again, she'd squashed his crush.

How would they come back from this and work together to catch the Coastline Strangler?

Jace muzzled any feelings for this woman and scrambled toward the door. "We're in here. We. Need. Air." He inhaled, but the smoke-infested oxygen caught. He coughed, burying his mouth and nose in his sleeve.

"We're coming." Something scraped against

the floor before a firefighter yanked open the door, running inside. "We got you. You're okay."

The muffled words behind the man's mask did little to still Jace's broken heart. How had he let another woman infiltrate the wall he'd built up throughout the past few years? Whatever had caused Scarlet's reaction toward him had to be brushed aside for now. She still required his protection. Wasting no time, Jace guided Scarlet from the room before hustling her outside.

They both gulped in the fresh air, doubling over.

"You okay?" he asked.

She nodded.

Taylor followed them out, helping a weakened Lewis.

Jace stepped closer. "What happened?"

Lewis wiped the perspiration off his face with his forearm. "Attack came from nowhere. I was sitting at my desk and heard shots. I went for my gun and ran in the gunfire's direction." He rubbed the back of his head. "Got clocked from behind."

"CLS got away. The shots killed poor Whitney. I've called in the coroners and paramedics." Taylor clenched her fists. "I also discovered listening devices planted throughout our station. When will this end?"

A firefighter walked from the building and approached. "The fire is out. Just a small one near your office, Constable Allen. Someone shoved a filing cabinet in front of your door. They obviously targeted you both."

Jace caught Scarlet's expression. Her terror-stricken eyes confirmed her fear.

"That's because he knows we're close to identifying him." Jace whisked dust from his uniform pants.

"You think this was CLS?" Taylor asked.

"Who else would it be? Of all the active cases we're working, this is the only one that screams desperation." While Jace knew other suspects could have committed this act, he believed in his gut it was CLS. Who else would be so brazen?

Scarlet removed an elastic from her pocket and rolled her hair into a bun at the nape of her neck. "When can we go back inside?"

The firefighter raised his hands. "You need to be checked out by paramedics first and the rooms aired out before I let anyone back in."

She turned to Jace. "I need to sketch. I was getting close. At least have someone grab my belongings. I can go to your place and do the work from there."

Was that really the reason, or was Scarlet wanting to distance herself from him? Something had happened back in that room, causing her to withdraw.

Had more memories returned? Did she remember their shaky relationship?

"I'll go get her things." The firefighter put his mask on and entered the building.

Jace's cell phone buzzed, and he checked the screen. "Gotta take this." He turned to Taylor. "Can you take Scarlet to my place and ensure it's locked up tight? Then keep watch. I'll be there shortly."

Jace walked away and hit Answer on his phone. "Constable Allen here."

"It's Colonel Maurier from the army. I understand you're inquiring about a roadside bombing from ten years ago."

"Yes. I believe a Kevin Vale was killed. Was he ever identified?"

Keyboard clicking sounded through the phone. "Just checking. My memory isn't what it used to be." A pause. "Ah, yes. I remember now. Explosion took out most of the team, including Kevin. A couple of others were severely injured. Wait." Another pause. "That's odd. The file only includes a coroner's report. The rest is redacted and sealed. Why do you ask?"

Jace curbed a huff as thunder thrashed his temples. "It coincides with a case I'm working on. Can you send me a copy of the report?" He stopped. The idea of a department leak crept through his body. "And please keep this inquiry between us. I can't explain why, but this needs the utmost discretion." He gave his email address.

"Understood. I'll get on it right away." Maurier hung up.

A tremor crept up Jace's back. Was Kevin Vale alive and the Coastline Strangler? If so, what was his secret identity? Jace glanced around. It could be anyone they knew. Anyone close to them.

Scarlet sat at Jace's dining room table overlooking his massive property and cliffs in the distance. Charlie played with his trucks in the backyard, racing them across the lawn while Marcy relaxed in an Adirondack chair, reading. The serenity of the scene washed over Scarlet after such a horrific event earlier. Her memory of the way she'd treated Jace in college shamed her, and she couldn't look him in the eye. She recalled how she'd suspected his crush, but she wasn't willing to date an arrogant, flirty football player, even though she was attracted to him, so she'd retreated from their shaky friendship. Could he forgive her for judging him back then? He'd changed into an amazing man.

The paramedics had checked her over and suggested she go to the hospital, but she'd refused. She was tired of hospitals, plus she needed to work on her age progression sketch. Identifying CLS was the task she was assigned to do, and she prided herself in her work. She knew that now.

The horror of the latest attack had brought her memories back until the point of Lila's interview and the identification of her killer. Why hadn't those last scenes also returned? Everything else had come back, including her feelings toward Jace in college, her angst over her mother's Alzheimer's diagnosis, all her forensic skills, her fractured faith in God and, most importantly...

The secret she withheld from everyone.

The rape Brandon Snow had inflicted on her when she tried to break up with him after she'd discovered his secret identity—his wife and kids. Scarlet's boss was right...she had changed after that incident, but had never shared it with anyone. Not even Olive, her sister and best friend. Shame prevented her from divulging her pain.

It was also the night her faith in God's protection had wavered. How could He have allowed such a thing to happen?

Scarlet tugged a strand of hair as heat traveled up her neck. The anger from the rape returned like it happened yesterday and not two years ago. She almost wished the memory had stayed hidden. Scarlet hated the person she'd turned into after that night. The terror had changed her. Molded her into something she despised.

But now, O Lord, thou art our father; we are the clay, and thou our potter; and we all are the work of thy hand.

Scarlet slumped her shoulders as the verse she'd memorized returned. Had God allowed her amnesia to wipe the anger from her mind?

To reshape and sculpt her into His image? Her personality had been restored these past few days after being suppressed for two years. Scarlet did not want to return to being that bitter person without joy.

Never again.

She hung her head.

Lord, forgive my bitterness. Forgive my anger toward You. I'm sorry. Mold me into the person You want me to be. I give my life back to You. Use it for Your glory, not mine. Bring back the memory of CLS's face so we can save more women from his destruction. Thank You for showing me You again. I love You.

Her restored identity washed over her as tears spilled down her cheeks and splatted on the table. Not tears of shame, but tears of renewal. Scarlet Wells had returned from the abyss.

And now she had a job to do.

She wiped her tears and swiped her tablet screen, bringing it to life.

CLS's young face stared back at her. She zoomed in on his eyes and studied her sketch of the killer's eyes.

They were the same, but different. Older.

Scarlet knew most faces aged in expected ways, and she would use that knowledge to sketch an older version of Kevin Vale. She researched his mother first and also reviewed her face closely. Old-school was her preferred method of forensic artistry, so Scarlet took out tracing paper from her bag and placed it over the picture on her tablet, then transferred it to a new page in her sketchbook.

Over time, eyes and their lids grow, widening. She erased portions of the eyes, then adjusted and aged them. After lengthening the lower part of the face, she expanded the lips over the teeth and barrel of the mouth. She drew the nose outward to show the normal growth as an adult and shaded around it. She thickened the eyebrows and added a modern hairstyle to the head.

Twenty minutes later, the front door opened and closed.

"Scarlet?" Jace yelled.

She set down her pencil and stood, bracing herself to face the man she cared for deeply. Would he ever forgive her earlier reaction? "In the dining room."

Approaching footsteps pounded on the tile.

Jace entered the room. "How's the sketch going?"

Scarlet held up her drawing. "Coming along. What did the military say about the bombing?"

"Case was redacted and sealed. He didn't know why, but he was able to get the coroner's report for me. I've sent it along to Dr. Drew and Dr. Parker. I want their opinions." Jace walked into the kitchen and returned seconds later with a bottle of water.

"Anything can happen. I remember once—"

She stopped, realizing her mistake. It wasn't the way she wanted to tell him her news.

He whirled around. "You have your memory back?"

She gestured to the chairs. "Take a seat. I need to talk to you."

His face blanched before he sat.

What worried him? Her returning memories?

She sat and reached for his hands. "I'm sorry for earlier. I didn't mean to react the way I did. I remember everything until Lila's interview. Not sure why that's still blocked."

He yanked his hands away. "So you recall how I treated you in college?"

She chewed her lip. "I remember how we treated *each other*. Jace, it's a two-way street. You're not that person any longer and neither am I. I've done so many things wrong in my life. Things I wish I could change."

He ran his thumb along her chin. "You're different since the fire this morning."

"I am. I've realized why God allowed these circumstances in my life to happen. He used my amnesia to cleanse me. Renew the old Scarlet and shape her into a stronger woman."

"I'm so glad." He paused. "I've missed our friendship, even though we fought most of the time."

She chuckled. "Let's not waste time on the past, okay?"

"Agreed. Let's start something new."

What did he mean by that? Something as in friendship—or more? She stared into his beautiful eyes. Oh, how she longed for more with him. He was the type of man she had prayed for all her life.

If only she could trust him with her secret.

She turned to look at her sketch, breaking their moment.

Time to get back to work. She wouldn't let her failed relationship impede identifying a killer.

"Scarlet, what is it you're not telling me?"

She swung her gaze back to his. "I can't—"

Pounding footsteps interrupted her words. Marcy flew into the room, out of breath. "Help! I can't find him!"

Jace bounded out of his chair. "Marcy, slow down. Where's Charlie?"

She crumbled to the floor. "He's gone."

"*What?*" An expression flashed across Jace's contorted face.

One she'd never seen on the man.

His son's disappearance haunted his mind.

Lord, help us find Charlie!

SEVENTEEN

Jace suppressed his anger at Charlie's abduction and brought his son's nanny to her feet. "We'll find him, Marcy." At least, he prayed it would happen. Fears from his kidnapping overpowered him and increased the pounding in his head. *God, please make it so. Don't take my son from me!*

"It's all my fault," she sobbed, her legs buckling.

Scarlet guided Marcy to a chair. "Tell us what happened."

Jace squared his shoulders, determination setting in, and he raised his index finger. "Just a sec. I need to get my team here to help scour the property." He quickly called Heller and requested backup, telling him to send Taylor from her cruiser out front to check the property, then clicked off. "Okay, go ahead."

Marcy hiccuped, her sobs increasing.

Scarlet rubbed the nanny's back. "Take a few

long breaths and then walk us through it. I'll get some water." She ran to the fridge and brought a bottle to Marcy.

Good thing Scarlet's calm demeanor had kicked into gear, because Jace struggled to hold in his panicked state. Had this been what his parents went through when they'd discovered he was taken? His galloping pulse and weakened limbs proved the unbelievable terror they must have suffered. He gripped the chair's back to steady himself and waited for Marcy's sobs to lessen.

"He...he was playing with his trucks, and my cell phone rang." Marcy took a sip of water before continuing. "It was the call I'd been waiting for—news on my mother's cancer—and I didn't want him to hear me, so I walked to the cliff and answered. My back was to him."

"Wait, you turned your back on my son when there's a killer targeting him?" Jace failed to keep the anger from his tone.

Marcy buried her face in her hands and once again sobbed. "I'm so sorry."

Scarlet squeezed his shoulder. "Not helping." She set a chair in front of Marcy and brought her into an embrace. "Shh...you had no way of knowing someone was watching. Perhaps he just wandered off."

His shoulders curled forward as remorse over his harsh words filled him. Scarlet was right. They didn't know for sure. He squatted in front of his beloved nanny. "I'm so sorry, Marcy. I shouldn't have said that. Can you forgive me?"

She lifted her gaze. "I know what happened to you at Charlie's age. I understand your anger."

Scarlet's knitted forehead silently questioned Marcy's statement.

He had to ignore it for now. "Tell me what happened next."

"When I finished the call—it was only a couple of minutes—I turned and he was gone. I searched all over the backyard and into the front but couldn't find him. Anywhere. Then I came here."

Jace's radio crackled.

"Allen, it's Lewis."

Jace pressed the button. "Go ahead."

"Couple things. So far, nothing from bartenders in the area. Also, the fire chief found a body in the mother's home. Appears to be Mrs. Brampton." He paused. "Sorry to hear about Charlie. Heller and I are here to help Taylor conduct the search of your property."

Jace stood. "Thanks for the update. We'll check the house in case Charlie came back inside using a different entrance."

He disconnected as doubt filled his mind. His gut told him his son was nowhere in the house.

Marcy stumbled into a standing position. "I'm going to help, too."

Jace realized trying to persuade the frantic

woman would be useless. Plus, the more help, the better.

The group conducted a thorough search—inside and out—and fifteen minutes later, Heller, Lewis, Taylor, Marcy and Scarlet gathered around Jace's surveillance monitors. He fast-forwarded through the footage.

"Stop!" Scarlet pointed. "There."

A masked man appeared, holding a limp Charlie in his grip. He skulked by the camera and looked back, staring at the lens as if taunting Jace. Then he crawled through a cut portion of the chain-link fence.

Jace slammed his hand down, immediately regretting his action, but the truth was evident.

His son had been taken.

He dropped his head and sobbed, years of pent-up fears taking over. Jace's panic room and high-tech security measures had failed him.

Jace was aware of the stats on abductions. *He* had failed his son, and now the sweet boy would pay the price.

"We'll find him." Scarlet squeezed his shoulder.

Lewis cleared his throat. "Let's get an Amber alert out immediately."

Jace popped his head up and wiped his tears, resolution girding his jaw. It was vital they act fast. The first forty-eight hours were the most important. "Yes. Lewis, you take care of that.

Marcy, can you tell him exactly what Charlie was wearing?"

She nodded. They moved to the side, whispering as she gave a description.

"Heller, we need to conduct a town-wide search. Can you get a party together? Bring in all the constables. Get a chopper in the air. Expenses don't matter. I'll cover everything. Get the media involved. I'm putting you in charge."

The constable nodded and left the room.

"What are you going to do?" Scarlet asked.

"I'm the parent. I need to stay here." As hard as it was, he recognized his best course of action was to excuse himself as the lead investigator. He was too emotionally attached and wouldn't make the right decisions.

Scarlet latched onto him. "I can help Heller search."

"No. You need to finish your sketch. It's important to identify CLS quickly. It will help find my son."

"What about me?" Taylor asked. "Do you want me to have a constable stationed in your laneway?"

Did he still trust in his own abilities to protect Scarlet? He required all officers out there looking for his son. Could he choose between Charlie and Scarlet? He moved his gaze to her.

"Jace, I'll be fine." She patted the Smith &

Wesson at her side. "You need the help in finding Charlie."

He turned to Taylor. "Grab the constables on foot patrol and search the beaches close to my property."

She nodded and ran from the room.

"I'm going to make some Earl Grey." Marcy left the equipment room.

Jace plunked himself in the chair and buried his head in his hands, all energy draining from his body. Tears threatened, but he kept them at bay.

Scarlet sat beside him and brought him into an embrace. "I'm sorry, Jace. Your officers are excellent at what they do."

"I feel so helpless."

"I understand. That's how I felt when I realized I couldn't remember CLS's face." She rubbed his back. "God will provide."

He retreated from her embrace and held both of her hands in his. "Can you pray?" His mind was too bogged down to put two sentences together, let alone a prayer.

She nodded and bowed her head. "Lord, we need Your powerful hand of protection. Wherever Charlie is, keep him safe. Wrap Your arms around him so he won't be scared. Put Your special touch on all the officers searching. Lead them directly to Charlie. Please be with Jace right now. Keep him safe under Your protective wings.

Give him strength. We pray all these things in Your precious name, amen."

Jace squeezed her hands. "I don't know what I would have done if you weren't here. Thank you."

"Tell me what Marcy meant by what happened to you at Charlie's age."

He let out an elongated sigh. "I've only shared this with Marcy. Not exactly sure why. Shame, maybe." He paused. "I was abducted at five years old."

"What?"

"My mom had just taken me to the school bus, and a few minutes later, my abductors pulled us over. They boarded the bus and only took me. My parents were targeted for their wealth." His heart rate accelerated as memories propelled him back into the past. "Even though I was only five, I remember it like it was yesterday."

"What happened? How did they find you?"

"Thankfully, my kidnappers were only in it for the money, and once my parents paid the ransom, they dropped me off at a nearby park and took off. Police never did catch them." Jace had suffered nightmares for years after his abduction.

"I'm sorry you went through that. No wonder you reacted as you did." She rubbed his hands before releasing them. "I understand now why you have a panic room and several phones. You had to protect your family."

He traced her face with his finger, stopping at her lips. "Scarlet, I need to tell you something." His cell phone rang, and he glanced at the screen. *Dr. Henry Drew.*

Why would he be calling? He hit the speaker-phone. "Dr. Drew, I'm here with Scarlet Wells. How can we help you?"

"Listen, I saw the Amber alert about Charlie, and I'm so sorry." The man's voice resonated sincere sympathies.

"Thank you."

"Unfortunately, that's not the only reason for this conversation. CLS called and told me where he left his latest victim."

"What? Why would he call you?" Scarlet asked.

Silence.

Jace checked to ensure the call hadn't dropped. "Dr. Drew? You still there?"

"I'm not sure why. I need you to meet me and Dr. Parker at Owl Bay Beach. Right away. It's of the utmost importance."

"I can't leave. My son is still out there."

"Jace, that's exactly why I'm calling you." The man's voice was garbled. Bad connection.

"What do you mean?" What did Charlie have to do with the latest victim?

"CLS sent me a picture. I'm forwarding it to you."

Seconds later, Jace's cell dinged. He brought up the photo.

It was of a woman's body positioned on the beach, and in the distance, the camera had caught a masked man holding a curly-haired blond boy.

Scarlet gasped. "Jace, go! Charlie could be there."

"Dr. Drew, I'm on my way." He didn't wait for an answer and ended the call. "I don't want to leave you here unprotected. I can't."

"I will be fine. I need to finish this sketch. Besides, Gail is close by if I need her."

Jace checked his Glock 17's chamber. "Call Lewis. Get constables to Owl Bay Beach. Now!" He sprinted from the room and out to his cruiser.

He prayed he'd make it before the Coastline Strangler took his son's life as a punishment for interfering in his so-called mission.

Scarlet's pulse thrashed in her ears. Ten minutes had passed since Jace left, and her muscles still remained tense. She'd called Doug and told him about Dr. Drew's call. There was nothing more to do other than pray and finish the sketch of CLS's face as quickly as possible. She picked up her pencil and studied what she'd accomplished so far. Almost there.

Scarlet tweaked the chin, brows and hair one more time before removing a fingerprint glass from her kit.

She studied the drawing of CLS closely

through the glass, checking for details. Scarlet needed to get this right—no room for errors.

She made a last touch and leaned back to look at her final sketch.

The familiar face plagued her mind. *Come on, memory, come back to me. Please, Lord!* She stood and paced the length of the dining room. *Think, Scarlet. Think.* Kevin Vale was someone she'd seen before, but she failed to put her finger on it.

Marcy walked to the table. "I brought you some tea and a chocolate cookie."

"Thank you. How are you doing?" Scarlet sat back down.

"Terrible. I love that boy and his father with all my heart. I would do anything for them." Marcy plunked herself into a chair across the table, staring into the backyard. "I just keep wishing I could turn back time and do things differently. If I had, Charlie would still be out there playing with the trucks he loves so much."

Scarlet reached across the table and rubbed the nanny's arm. "Marcy, this is *not* your fault. CLS is devious and smart. He's proven to be able to evade surveillance equipment easily in the past few days. He's been under our noses the entire time. I just can't figure out where I know him from." She pushed her sketch to the middle of the table, turning it around to show Marcy.

The different angle of CLS's face triggered a memory.

Scarlet and Marcy bolted out of their chairs simultaneously.

"It's Aiden Parker, the deputy coroner." Dread tingled throughout Scarlet's body. "And Jace is on his way to see him right now. He's walking into a trap."

Marcy turned ashen, and she sank back into her seat, fear etched on her contorted face. "You have to warn him."

"How far away is Owl Bay Beach?"

"Twenty minutes."

Scarlet checked her watch. He'd almost be there by now. She snatched her phone from the table and punched in his number.

"Scarlet, I'm just arriving at the beach." Jace's voice sounded surprisingly calm.

"Jace! Listen closely, it's a trap!"

"What—say? You're—breaking—up."

Scarlet gripped her cell tighter. "CLS is—"

The call dropped.

No, Lord!

"Marcy, is there a vehicle I can use?" Scarlet grabbed her nine-millimeter, stuffed it into her waistband and dropped a pocketknife into her pocket. A pencil and sketch pad wouldn't help with this situation, so she wanted to be prepared. "I have to get there fast."

The nanny ran to a cupboard and took a key

fob from a hook, handing it to her. "Take Jace's Jeep. Be careful."

"I will. I'll call Gail on the way." Scarlet raced from the house.

Praying the entire time.

Jace eyeballed his cell phone. Dead. The reception in this area was faulty at best, but he'd forgotten to charge his battery. *Stupid!* What had Scarlet been trying to tell him? Had she identified CLS?

He parked beside the coroner's van and stepped from his cruiser. He stopped short at the sight before him.

Dr. Henry Drew's arm dangled out the driver's side window, blood dripping from his fingertips.

Jace's pulse spiked, and he drew his weapon, approaching the van with his Glock raised. "Police!"

Only the waves slapping the shoreline answered.

Jace peeked inside the van.

Dr. Drew's carotid artery had been severed. The man was gone.

Scarlet's broken words repeated in his brain. Was she saying this was a trap?

His muscles tensed, and he pointed his weapon in all directions, glancing around the area.

"Daddy!"

Jace pivoted at the sound of his son's desperate cry.

Charlie sat on a large piece of driftwood in front of a roaring fire, hands and feet tied. The sun was setting on the horizon. A woman's body was positioned close by in the normal CLS fashion. However, the killer was nowhere to be found.

Jace sprinted across the sand toward his son. He had to reach him before CLS returned. Jace stopped a few feet shy of Charlie and holstered his weapon. He didn't want to scare him any more.

He crouched in front of his son and gathered him into his arms. "It's okay, bud. I have you now."

"No, Daddy. Bad man. Careful."

A twig snapped behind him.

Jace pivoted.

And stared into the eyes of the Coastline Strangler—Dr. Aiden Parker, aiming a rifle at them.

The man smirked. "See, I told you I'd get you all. I only hated that I had to kidnap your son to catch your attention. Seems you and Miss Scarlet are hard to kill."

Jace steeled his jaw. "You will never get to my son or Scarlet. Not even over my dead body." He leveled his Glock at the menacing coroner and blocked his son's view.

Aiden let out a growling laugh. "That's where

you're wrong. You see, your love is on her way here right now."

"What? How do you know that?"

He cocked his head. "I've been watching you all."

"How?"

"Living on the streets as a teenager taught me so much. I'm a chameleon. I can change my appearance quickly and adapt. Also, my drone patrols the skies. No one suspects a coroner would know much about surveillance equipment, but you see, I served in the army for a short period... until the bombing that took a bully's life. I was outside the vehicle when it hit."

He looked away, as if remembering the moment. When he turned back, his eyes had darkened. "I watched him die and burn beyond recognition. Oh, I could have saved him, but I was tired of his attitude. Tired of everything. I was ready to give up my army career, but then an idea hit me. I could kill that weasel of a man Kevin Vale and begin a new life. One that didn't have bullies or vixen women in it. I put my dog tags on my fellow officer. I took his and buried them in the desert. Later, I anonymously fed the media the bully's story, casting blame on the army and made it look like the man deserted."

"That's why they sealed the records. But how did you hide?"

"Easy. I walked away from the vehicle, and

when I stumbled upon a farmer, I pretended to have amnesia. He helped me to find someone to change my appearance and get me a new identity. I started over in my new career. During my time in the army, I learned about bombs, drones, hacking into video feeds. Everything. I've tapped into your station's equipment and at your house." He stepped closer. "I saw Miss Scarlet leave in your Jeep."

Jace raised his gun higher. "Don't take another step." He took one hand off his weapon and tugged Charlie closer to him, like a mother bird protecting her babies under her wings. He would do anything to protect his son and Scarlet.

It was at that moment he realized he was topsy-turvy in love with Scarlet Wells and wanted her in his life. He had released the hold Rene's betrayal held on him and no longer feared to love again. Peace bathed him in God's presence. His trust reemerged stronger in the One who allowed things to happen, to remold and reshape. He realized Christians only had to let *Him* be the sculptor, not them. *Lord, I surrender everything to you and trust You, right here, right now.*

Jace only hoped he'd be able to tell Scarlet how he felt. He must keep Aiden talking. Stall him. Scarlet would have called in his team by now. "You killed my boss."

"I had to shut him up. Clever, huh, how I snuck in right under your noses and set up the bomb?"

"How did you do it?"

"Patience. Plus, I knew where your cameras were. I waited for the opportune time, when you were in debrief and most of the firefighters were sleeping. I acted quickly."

"How did you get access to our station so easily?"

"You never figured that one out, did you?" Aiden sneered. "I was secretly dating Whitney."

Jace shifted his stance. "She was the leak?"

"She knew nothing. I convinced her to keep our relationship a secret. Told her I'm a private person. I used my access to your building to plant devices." He gazed at the water. "But she's smart and figured it out. Had to eliminate her when I attacked the station."

Jace thought back to all CLS's criminal activities since Scarlet arrived. Being a coroner, the man had easy access to the hospital, medical records and drugs. No wonder he'd gotten away with it so easily.

"You're pure evil." Jace stole a peek at the woman positioned on the sand. "Who's she?"

Aiden turned his gaze back, his eyes narrowing. "Another vixen."

"Why kill Dr. Drew?"

"He caught me trying to delete the coroner's report you had emailed us." He groaned. "Tragic, really. He taught me everything and was my friend. However, I couldn't let him stop me."

"Why did you—"

"Enough chitchat. Time to prepare for Miss Scarlet's arrival." He gestured toward a nearby tree. "I thought of everything."

Jace followed his movement.

A jerrican sat next to the oak.

The Coastline Strangler was going to use Scarlet's fear of fire to eliminate them all.

"How did you know about that?"

"Told you. I'm a talented man who has too much time on his hands."

Jace took a step and raised his gun higher. "I will not let you do this."

Charlie let out a pained grunt.

Jace turned.

His son doubled over on the log, clearly in distress.

Jace took a step and let his guard down for a second.

CLS pistol-whipped him at the back of the head. His vision blackened before he crumbled to the ground.

Scarlet took a turn too fast, and the Jeep's tires caught the soft gravel on the side of the roadway. She jerked the wheel back, straightening the vehicle. *Pay attention.* Her cell phone rang from where she had placed it in the holder. She stole a peek at the screen. *Unknown caller.* She hit Answer. "Scarlet here."

"It's time for you to join the party." His undistorted voice held sarcasm.

"What do you want from us, Aiden? Or should I call you Kevin Vale?"

"Ah…so you figured out who I am."

"You will not get away with this." Scarlet sped up and took the beach exit ramp.

He clucked his tongue. "Watch me. Look at the picture I'm sending."

Her phone dinged. She quickly switched to the photo.

Charlie and Jace were tied and gagged, sitting on a large piece of driftwood.

She cried out.

"That's right. I have them both. All we need is you. By the way, I called in a false lead on Charlie's whereabouts to the police and diverted them away from here. They're not coming. You contact them and I will know about it. That clear?"

She gritted her teeth. "Perfectly."

"See you soon." The evil CLS ended the call.

Scarlet banged the wheel. How could she get help without tipping him off? *Think!* An idea formed, and she yanked the vehicle to the side of the road, snatching up her cell phone. She opened the back and searched for a listening device. Nothing. Her thought was a risky one, but she had to try. She dialed Jace's private cell phone and prayed Marcy would hear it. One ring. Two. Three. "Come on, pick up!"

"Hello?" The nanny's weakened voice exposed her worry.

"Listen to me carefully. I can't call the police, but you can with this phone. I'm praying Aiden doesn't know about Jace's other number. You need to tell Constable Taylor the tip they received on Charlie is false. Tell them CLS is Aiden, and he's got Charlie and Jace at Owl Bay Beach. Forwarding a picture." She swiped the screen and texted the photo. "Hurry. You're our only hope."

"On it." Marcy's earlier tone changed from angst to one of resolution. "Be careful. I'm praying." She disconnected.

Scarlet maneuvered the Jeep back onto the road and sped toward the two men she loved.

Seven minutes later, she parked beside Jace's cruiser and the coroner's van in the beach's parking lot. Unleashing her weapon, she exited the vehicle and darted over to the van, where she found Dr. Drew dead. Scarlet withheld her anger toward Aiden Parker at yet another horrific act. She would release her outrage on him at the appropriate time.

Smoke filled the air, and she studied the beach.

A bonfire blazed near the shoreline. Something told her this was part of Aiden's villainous plan.

Lord, give me strength to overcome my fears.

She inhaled a deep breath and ran toward the fire. Something she'd never thought she'd do.

She stopped when she found the bonfire. The scene before her knocked the breath from her, and she struggled to inhale. Jace and Charlie were gagged and tied, slumped on a log. Feet bound.

She realized the absent Aiden wouldn't be far. Time to escape. An odor paralyzed her limbs. What was that smell?

Gas. Not good.

"Jace!" she yelled and sprinted to his side, squatting in front of him. She set her gun down and touched the blood dripping from his temple. She loosened the ropes at his wrists.

He stirred and moaned before opening his eyes.

"I'm here," she whispered.

His eyes widened, and he muffled a cry, shaking his head in another direction.

"Well, it's about time you joined the party." A menacing voice came from behind her, followed by the sound of a rifle shot. "The next bullet won't miss."

Scarlet winced as realization struck her. His army background would beat her limited shooting experience, so she had to outwit him. She tucked her gun into her ankle boot and covered it with her slacks, all the while staring into Jace's eyes. She prayed he'd get her meaning.

His gaze drifted downward at her pant leg, and he gave a slight nod.

She stood and turned, peering into the eyes of the Coastline Strangler.

Eyes that were more daunting in person than on paper.

She braced her arms at her sides. "Let. Them. Go."

"Never. You all need to pay the price for interfering." He raised his weapon.

"Let Charlie go. He's an innocent boy. It's me you want." She held her hands up. "I surrender. I give myself for their lives."

Jace moaned behind her.

She ignored him. "Come on. You know it's me you want. After all, I probably fit your profile of these vixen women."

"Hardly. Yes, you kind of resemble my dear old mom, but you don't hang out in bars and on beaches, flirting with men."

"Is that what she did? Is that why you picked these women?" She looked at his latest victim, positioned on the ground beside the fire, seashell necklace strategically placed around the ligatures on her neck, lips painted red.

"Mother loved to take me to the beach just to use me as a tool for picking up men. One would come along and she'd leave me by myself. Told me not to move or I'd get the whip on my behind." His eyes darkened, turning more eerie than before. "She'd go off with them, and I would hunt for seashells. They comforted me."

"So, the necklaces on your victims were to comfort them in their dying moments? How sick are you?" *Come on, team, get here quick. We need you.*

His expression softened. "After everything she did, I still loved her. I desired to add a token of that love on my victims."

"But you killed your mother in that drone strike. Why?"

"You were getting too close. Besides, it was time for her to pay for everything. That no-good rich husband of hers couldn't even save her."

"Is that why you started killing again? After she got married?" Scarlet shifted her position, bending at the knees slightly and putting herself in an attack stance.

"Smart girl."

"Tell me, why did you kill Ian, and why bring Violet into everything?"

"That's easy. Dear old Violet was ready to out my drug of choice. I wanted to make her pay, and it was a way to get to Jace." Aiden bent down to his victim and adjusted a seashell. "Ian, on the other hand, was a tragedy. He was my best friend, but he saw me the night I killed—or thought I killed—Lila Canfield."

It now made sense. Well, sense in Aiden's mind. All these people were out to spoil his mission. Stop him from ridding the island of his "vixens." Sick.

Aiden once again raised his weapon. "Show me your gun."

She held out her hands. "I rarely carry one." Movement sounded behind her. Was Jace free of his bindings yet? She had to give him more time.

Charlie whimpered.

Lord, keep the little guy calm.

"Okay, we're going to get this party started." Aiden reached behind another log and picked up an item.

A jerrican.

No, Lord!

"That's right. I know about the accident that killed Becky. You see, after you just wouldn't die, I dug deep and discovered everything I could about you. Found an article from your childhood, when your friend died. Thought it would be a fitting way for you as well. Your punishment for interfering." He stuffed the gun into his waistband and pressed diesel through the pump, spraying it in her direction.

She screamed.

"I've soaked this entire area. You can't escape."

Scarlet felt motion behind her. Jace had freed himself and slowly eased up her pant leg, removing her gun.

Sirens blared in the distance.

Marcy had called in the team.

Aiden's eyes narrowed. "How did you—"

"You're not the only one with tricks up their sleeves." Scarlet prayed, asking God for protection and strength. Strength to face her fears. "Surrender. It's over."

"They can't save you. It's too late." Aiden pulled a gun from his waistline and a dart from his front pocket, inserting it into the chamber. "This will help you sleep and ensure you don't escape." He dug a lighter out, flicking it at the same time he aimed the weapon in her direction.

No! They had to act fast. She wiggled her fingers at her sides, hoping Jace would get her signal.

The slight tug on her pants proved he did.

"Now, Jace!" Scarlet dived to the right, moving away from the possible gunfight.

Jace fired. His shot hit Aiden in the shoulder.

He screamed and fell to the ground, dropping the lighter. Flames erupted, sending a blaze in every direction.

Blocking their escape.

Shouts from across the beach drew closer. She prayed for the constables to make it in time.

A ring of fire circled Charlie and Jace, but their ankles were still bound. She had to get to them, even if it meant risking her life. Scarlet mustered up courage and bolted toward them, leaping through the flames. She dropped and rolled to rid herself of any embers, then scrambled to them. She removed her pocketknife and cut their ankle ropes.

Charlie whimpered, and Scarlet lifted him from the log. "I've got you, bud."

Jace staggered to his feet. "Scarlet, move!" He raised the weapon.

She turned.

Aiden eased himself up, pointing his rifle at them.

Scarlet vaulted to the right.

Jace fired. This time, the shot met its target.

Aiden collapsed.

Constables raced toward them, shouting.

Doug reached them first, spraying the contents of a fire extinguisher into the inferno. Not that it would eliminate the blazing flames entirely, but it would help them escape what would have been their fiery grave.

Scarlet leaped through the flames with Jace behind her. They distanced themselves from the fire before she set Charlie on the sand and patted him down for embers.

Frank and Gail circled around to the other side and tugged Aiden's body from the scene.

"Charlie!" Marcy ran toward them, holding out her arms. "I'll take him to the paramedics." She lifted the boy and moved back to the ambulance.

Firefighters hustled all around them to put out the fire.

The adrenaline left Scarlet's body, and she dropped to the ground, shaking.

Jace crouched beside her and enveloped her into an embrace. "You saved us."

He smelled of smoke, but she didn't care. She nuzzled deeper into his arms. "I would do anything for you, Jace."

"Scarlet, I want you in my life. Permanently."

She stiffened at his intent. "Will you after you learn about the secret I've kept from everyone, including my sister?"

He released his hold. "What do you mean?"

"I finally remember everything." She hesitated, but only for a second. She had to clear the air. "Two years ago, I discovered my boyfriend of eight months was leading a double life. He had a wife and child I'd known nothing about. I felt shame at myself for not being able to read the man. I was trained to detect when someone was lying, but I failed to see it in him."

He rubbed her cheek with his thumb. "I understand. My wife cheated on me with a coworker. I get it."

"There's more." She heaved out a sigh. "When I tried to break it off, he—he raped me." Tears escaped, tumbling down her face. "I'm so ashamed, I never told anyone."

Jace brought her back into his arms. "I'm sorry you went through that."

Could she tell him her true feelings? *Do it.* "Jace Allen, I had a crush on you in college."

Once again, he leaned back, grinning. "What? I thought you hated me."

She ran her finger down his cheek, stopping at his chin dimple. "Never."

"I had a crush on you, too, but we always fought."

"We acted like children, being mean to the one we were interested in. It kept our feelings hidden and us apart."

"Exactly. For too long." He eyed her lips. "Scarlet Wells, I love you."

Her heart stuttered. "Ditto."

He brought her closer, touching her lips with his in a gentle, romantic kiss.

A kiss that would remain etched in her memory—forever.

EPILOGUE

One year later

Scarlet adjusted her flowing white wedding dress and followed Charlie Allen down the red carpet laid across the sandy beach toward the shoreline. He tossed rose petals on each side of their royal rug. No seashells here. She had asked the boy who'd stolen her heart to be both a flower boy and ring bearer. He'd hopped with joy, accepting his dual role in his father's wedding.

Scarlet's raven hair was swept into a soft French twist at the nape of her neck, with tiny red roses tucked into the folds. Her bouquet matched the petals on the sand, along with the flowers in her updo. A tiara at the top of her head completed her wedding ensemble, making her feel like a princess. She grinned at the man waiting beside the trellis positioned in front of the waves.

His eyes matched the ocean, stealing her breath away.

Like they did every time his gaze found hers.

In the days after the Coastline Strangler was revealed, the small community of Coral Bay rallied together to comfort each other at the discovery of one of their own being a serial killer. Aiden Parker had succumbed to his gunshot wounds. His death sent a shock wave through the town. One of both sadness and relief. The women of the island were once again safe, but it took months for the town to come back from the deception of one of their own residents. Aiden had fooled them all.

Jace's leader had promoted him officially after all his heroic actions. He was now Deputy Chief Jace Allen. His coworkers, who were once jealous of his abilities, now looked up to him.

All of Scarlet's memories returned, and she made amends with those she'd wronged during the two years after her rape. She had only shared the tragic events of that night with her family and her boss, asking for their forgiveness for keeping it a secret. Scarlet discovered Brandon Snow had been diagnosed with terminal cancer, so to protect his family and not cause them further heartache, Scarlet decided not to pursue any legal actions. She'd finally moved on from that frightful night.

Jace, Charlie and Scarlet had formed an unbreakable bond after the day Aiden tried to take their lives. Jace and Scarlet dated for six months before he popped the question, each traveling back and forth between their homes. Scarlet left her official role as forensic artist in Whitehorse and opened a freelance business. She wanted to spend more time with her new family—Jace, Charlie and Marcy—so they turned the cottage on Jace's property into an office for her to take on cases helping police identify victims as well as training up-and-coming artists.

She would officially move into her new home on the beach's cliff after their wedding.

A seagull squawked overhead as the waves crashed on the shoreline against the red-orange sun, kissing the horizon and sparkling on the water. She smiled.

Even though the beaches on this island had seen heartache, joy still radiated in their beauty.

Scarlet winked at her sister as she passed by their row. Her mother and father sat beside Olive. Even though Scarlet knew her mother's memory was mostly gone, Evelyn and Carson Wells beamed from ear to ear at their daughter. A tear escaped as she remembered the moment when she felt the connection with what her mother must have experienced when her memories failed. Scarlet wiped it away and moved onward. She would visit her parents as much as possible.

Scarlet stepped onto the makeshift stage and stood facing the man of her dreams.

Jace winked and leaned closer, placing a kiss on her cheek. "You look beautiful."

She fingered the rose on his suit jacket lapel. "You don't look so shabby yourself, handsome."

"Time to get married!" Charlie yelled, jumping in between them.

The small crowd burst into laughter.

Ten minutes later, after Scarlet and Jace had shared their vows, the pastor cleared his throat. "I now pronounce you husband and wife. Jace, you may kiss your bride."

Jace took Scarlet into his arms and dipped her as if in a dance. He leaned closer and kissed her deeply.

Once again stealing her breath.

Scarlet silently thanked God for her husband—her hero.

Most of all, she praised Him for walking through the fire with her and restoring her memory, shaping her into the woman she was meant to be.

A sculpted work of her Father.

* * * * *

*If you liked this story from Darlene L. Turner,
check out her previous
Love Inspired Suspense books:*

Border Breach
Abducted in Alaska
Lethal Cover-Up
Safe House Exposed

*Available now from Love Inspired Suspense!
Find more great reads at
www.LoveInspired.com.*

Dear Reader,

Thank you so much for joining me on Scarlet and Jace's roller-coaster adventure! Action hounded them at every corner. Thankfully they had each other to help overcome the difficulties they faced. I can't imagine what Scarlet must have gone through when she lost her memory. However, in the end they both grew stronger in their faiths when they allowed God to sculpt their identities and mold them into whom He wanted them to be—children of the King. Isn't that what our Father wants from us, too?

I enjoyed creating the fictional town of Coral Bay, British Columbia. I loosely based it on the real town of Oak Bay—a picturesque community on Vancouver Island.

I'd love to hear from you. You can contact me through my website, www.darlenelturner.com, and also sign up for my newsletter to receive exclusive subscriber giveaways. Thanks for reading my story.

God bless,
Darlene L. Turner

Get 4 FREE REWARDS!

We'll send you 2 FREE Books plus 2 FREE Mystery Gifts.

FREE
Value Over
$20

Both the **Harlequin® Special Edition** and **Harlequin® Heartwarming™** series feature compelling novels filled with stories of love and strength where the bonds of friendship, family and community unite.

YES! Please send me 2 FREE novels from the Harlequin Special Edition or Harlequin Heartwarming series and my 2 FREE gifts (gifts are worth about $10 retail). After receiving them, if I don't wish to receive any more books, I can return the shipping statement marked "cancel." If I don't cancel, I will receive 6 brand-new Harlequin Special Edition books every month and be billed just $4.99 each in the U.S or $5.74 each in Canada, a savings of at least 17% off the cover price or 4 brand-new Harlequin Heartwarming Larger-Print books every month and be billed just $5.74 each in the U.S. or $6.24 each in Canada, a savings of at least 21% off the cover price. It's quite a bargain! Shipping and handling is just 50¢ per book in the U.S. and $1.25 per book in Canada.* I understand that accepting the 2 free books and gifts places me under no obligation to buy anything. I can always return a shipment and cancel at any time. The free books and gifts are mine to keep no matter what I decide.

Choose one: ☐ **Harlequin Special Edition**
(235/335 HDN GNMP)

☐ **Harlequin Heartwarming**
Larger-Print
(161/361 HDN GNPZ)

Name (please print)

Address   Apt. #

City   State/Province   Zip/Postal Code

Email: Please check this box ☐ if you would like to receive newsletters and promotional emails from Harlequin Enterprises ULC and its affiliates. You can unsubscribe anytime.

Mail to the Harlequin Reader Service:
IN U.S.A.: P.O. Box 1341, Buffalo, NY 14240-8531
IN CANADA: P.O. Box 603, Fort Erie, Ontario L2A 5X3

Want to try 2 free books from another series! Call 1-800-873-8635 or visit www.ReaderService.com.

*Terms and prices subject to change without notice. Prices do not include sales taxes, which will be charged (if applicable) based on your state or country of residence. Canadian residents will be charged applicable taxes. Offer not valid in Quebec. This offer is limited to one order per household. Books received may not be as shown. Not valid for current subscribers to the Harlequin Special Edition or Harlequin Heartwarming series. All orders subject to approval. Credit or debit balances in a customer's account(s) may be offset by any other outstanding balance owed by or to the customer. Please allow 4 to 6 weeks for delivery. Offer available while quantities last.

Your Privacy—Your information is being collected by Harlequin Enterprises ULC, operating as Harlequin Reader Service. For a complete summary of the information we collect, how we use this information and to whom it is disclosed, please visit your privacy notice located at corporate.harlequin.com/privacy-notice. From time to time we may also exchange your personal information with reputable third parties. If you wish to opt out of this sharing of your personal information, please visit readerservice.com/consumerschoice or call 1-800-873-8635. **Notice to California Residents**—Under California law, you have specific rights to control and access your data. For more information on these rights and how to exercise them, visit corporate.harlequin.com/california-privacy.

HSEHW22

COUNTRY LEGACY COLLECTION

19 FREE BOOKS IN ALL!

Cowboys, adventure and romance await you in this new collection! Enjoy superb reading all year long with books by bestselling authors like Diana Palmer, Sasha Summers and Marie Ferrarella!

Visit
ReaderService.com
Today!

As a valued member of the Harlequin Reader Service, you'll find these benefits and more at ReaderService.com:

- Try 2 free books from any series
- Access risk-free special offers
- View your account history & manage payments
- Browse the latest Bonus Bucks catalog